The Leather, the I

MW01101369

Dream Big Publishing
Byron Center, MI

Dream Big Publishing
A publication of Dream Big Publishing
Byron Center MI
Copyright 2016 by Ky Rose
All rights reserved, including the right of reproduction in
whole or in part in any form.
Dream Big Publishing is a registered trademark of
Dream Big Publishing.
Manufactured in the United States of America
All rights reserved.
People's photo © Bigstock.com

Summary: Michael Stateman is excited for his Senior year of high school. He's finally single, or so he thought, has a certain someone got him distracted? He feels on top of the world leading his football team into a challenging season, reaching for another sectional title. But just as Michael starts to let go of the past, it seems to only make things more difficult. In one moment his whole world changes, leaving him feeling abandoned, while trying to make life choices about his future. As he reaches out for the only one left, his mom, she seems to disappear. Taking everything and everyone into consideration. Suddenly reconnected with a friendly face, Michael is reminded he isn't the only one the past has affected. Can they work together to move on? Or will the past, and a certain other individual keep them apart?

[1. Young Adult – Fiction 2. Romance, 3. Comedy]
978-1530691401
Ky Rose
Copyright 2016 by Ky Rose
Smashwords Edition
All rights reserved.

Dedication

I'd like to dedicate my first book to my parents, Greg and Dania, for raising me to have enough courage to follow my dreams. The only two people who understand how writing is my escape. I'd also like to dedicate this book to my late grandma, Rose (may she rest in peace). Before she left for her forever home she graciously left me with her gift of creativity.

Chapter One

It's going to be a good year, it's my senior year, and my friends and I are definitely going to go out with a bang. This is going to be a year that's going to tell a story and us; the ones who leave behind the legacy. We plan on writing a new chapter, one that the younger kids will look back on and read over and over, so they can get an idea of how the legends did it. This is going to be a year to dominate and have seniority over everyone else here, and the thought of it never sounded so good.

"Michael if you don't hurry you're going to be late!" my mother calls from downstairs.

"I'll be down in a second."

"NOW please!" I grab my football practice clothes and check my reflection in the mirror one last time. My shaggy brown hair is hanging lose as well as my clothes, for some reason I lost weight over the summer, not that I needed to, now I just happen to be more toned and am finally fully rocking six pack abs.

I head down the stairs taking them two at a time.

"Mom I promise I'm not going to be late." I approach the island in our kitchen and grab a banana.

"I don't want you starting this year off on a bad note; you have a lot riding with all the football scholarships and academics."

"I promise I won't blow this for us." I smile and give her a kiss on the cheek. She looks more relieved.

"Always being the man of the house." She smiles at me.

"Yes ma'am." I turn and head out to my truck. It's just been my mother and I for about half a year. My father is currently in the military and has been over in Iraq. It hasn't been very easy on mom and me.

My mom's a short lady about 5' 5 with short blond hair, I look like my dad. She's always been the strict parent, however since Dad's been gone she's let everything go. I think she's just more stressed and doesn't have time to worry or sweat the small stuff anymore. At times she acts like everything is okay and we're a happy family and others she caves. I haven't quite figured out how to help her through the tough times, but I'm trying.

My mother has never really let her feelings show. She smiles, and cries and laughs like every other human being but I've never seen a full deep belly laugh, or crocodile tears that never stop flowing, until about a year ago. Then the emotions with mom ran wild, and they still are to this day. And no it's not menopause.

I had an older brother Max, he was about a year in half older than I. He chose to be a Marine, and right after he graduated he was sent overseas. After about four months of him being gone we got the terrible news that he had been killed in action due to him and his squad running into a roadside bomb.

That was nine months ago, ever since mother doesn't mind breaking down in front of me. Not that I can say I blame her. When I'm alone I tend to break down myself. It still doesn't seem real to me, Max and I weren't only brothers, we were best friends. He was my confidant and the one person who knows every little thing and secret about me, he knew things not even our parent's know.

Mother was so happy when I decided I wanted to go to college. The only problem is she knows we're tight for money. So she's pushing and making sure I do everything I can this year to get as many scholarships as possible. Not that I blame her, I know she only wants the best for me.

We live in Southport, North Carolina. It's a small town so I've got to do really well this year both on and off the field in order to get noticed. It's my ticket to getting out of here. Although I already know some smaller schools are looking at me for football. I love the sport almost as much as I love my family. When I'm on the field I see nothing but the players and the ball. I'm completely in my element. On the field is the only place I really feel at home, even more than being here with mom. And I'm lucky because I'm good. I've been the starting quarterback for our school since freshman year. It just comes naturally to me.

Southport's not a bad town by any means, everybody knows everybody and we all have each other's backs, but unless you plan to teach, go into real-estate, become a banker, or like doing the odd jobs—like mine currently—lawn moving, yard work, and plumbing, there's just not a lot here. It's a cozy and quaint town that I feel I've just outgrown.

As I drive to school I think about what kind of field I'd like to study in college. It'd probably help if I thought more about which college I'd like to go to, but I figure I've got time for that.

I get to school, park and immediately see Kevin, one of my best guy friends. I get all my stuff together and get out of the truck.

"Kevin."

"Michael" We slap hands, and size each other up. "Dude you got buff."

"Thanks, and you got." I look him over "Shaggier hair."

"Awe, touché." Kevin's about 6'1 with blond hair that flops when he runs. He's a lean mean football machine as the ladies would say. Even though Kevin and I are close we didn't see each other much over the summer, my summer happened to be a little pre occupied with work and a certain someone. I actually didn't see any of the guys over the summer.

"So which girl you think you're going to go after since you're a free man?" I smile. A free man is so true. I had actually been dating Jasmine Hinkle, who is also in our class. We started dating the second day of freshman year and broke up the very end of this past May. To be exact we had been together two years and nine months. I've only been single for less than three months (sort of I guess) and I actually don't mind.

"I guess we'll just have to see, and you?" I smirk; okay maybe there's a girl. Her name is Avery Carson and we basically hung out all summer. It was two weeks after school let out we were both on the beach and it was late. I was sitting over by my rocks where my brother and I use to sit and talk all the time. I was by myself and having a beer—dad's old supply from the garage—don't want them to go to complete waste. Anyways just reminiscing after a long hard day of work. She came over not knowing I was there and started yelling and throwing rocks into the ocean. I startled her when I approached and asked if she was okay. Knowing Avery and I's history I can't believe I even attempted to make sure she was fine, but I'm a decent guy like that, and looking back, I'm glad I did.

Avery and I have always fought; like school debates, we always try and make it extremely hard for the other person to win. Or over politics, or which foods are healthy which are not. It doesn't matter what, we've just always been against each other. We have never agreed on anything and basically try to avoid one another, except all these years we somehow always end up in the same class. We just never understood each other. But this past summer somehow we got to talking and everything just flowed from there. We spent the whole summer together, even though we didn't do anything. We actually just talked and didn't fight. It was crazy and really nice. No one knew, none of our friends, or families, it was just our secret. Basically late at night I would sneak over to her house and we'd sit outside on her lawn for hours. Sometimes we'd talk and sometimes we'd just lay there and look at the stars. I guess it was nice to be in each other's company.

However, with school starting back up we decided it would be best to just drop it, we were just a summer fling if that's even what you could call it. Everyone in the school world knows we're from two separate worlds and it would just never work.

I'm what most girls call "the tall, dark and handsome." I'm 6'3 and have the athletic build, with brown eyes and shaggy brown hair. I'm the quarterback for the football team, co-captain of the basketball team and a member of the track team who finally won a first sectional championship. I'm smart, hardworking and outgoing with my group of guys. And believe it or not, I'm known as the one of the nicest guys in the whole school. I pretty much talk to any clique (well almost any, I do tend to stay away from the druggy group aka Avery's group) and have friends from every class, freshmen on up. I'm very simple, down to earth, and polite to everyone I meet. All the girls like me because even when I was dating Jasmine, I would still talk to other girls and be kind. Plus, I hated seeing a girl being treated without respect and usually I'd step in. Believe it or not that happens a lot in this community, mainly because everyone's afraid if they break up they won't find someone else. So they just put up with each other's crap, I know I did. I mean not abusive crap, but Jasmine and I's relationship wasn't so great.

But then there's Avery. She has long black hair that she always curls with all the tips dyed purple. She's smart, but hangs out with the wrong crowd, the ones who smoke and do the drugs, although she claims she's never done either. She's shy and really doesn't like to be bothered most of the time. She also has a tendency to have a nasty attitude when she wants too. She's not very social and in which I am. We don't see anything on the same page, and have no common interests. We really are opposites, but somehow over this summer when we were together we could talk about anything, but sports, just because she knows absolutely nothing about them. It surprised us both because all these years of high school we've kind of despised each other, although I'm not sure why. Who knows maybe we've both finally grown up?

So I guess we'll just see how this first week of school goes and take things one day at a time. I really like talking to Avery and she's easy on the eyes, I'm just not sure I'm ready for a relationship, after all my last one was pretty long, and it's my senior year.

Kevin however is always on the hunt for a girl; the fun of it for him is of course the hunt. Once he finds one he never stays with them. In all the years I've known Kevin I've never seen him have a relationship that's lasted more than 3 months.

"I'm thinking Nancy Douglass; she's looking hot this year." He says pulling me back to our current conversation. I glance around and my eyes finally find Nancy who's walking into school, not bad looking he's right. She looks more mature and has her thick red hair highlighted and I'm guessing she learned how to use a straightener like every other girl in this school, because her hair actually looks tame for once. For the record I only know what a straightener is because Jasmine used one all the time and I would occasionally watch her get ready. Nancy has been one of those girls who tries to fit in with every group but it never works because she's never herself. She tries way too hard and to be honest most of us don't even really know who she is. I'm not even sure the girl has any "real" friends.

"Well, good luck with that. Come on let's go find everyone else." We head towards the school doors. Once inside everyone seems to be buzzing about, all excited to see everyone and share how their summers went and to see who has the bragging rights of having the best and worst summer.

"There she is." Kevin punches my arm; sure enough Nancy's standing against the lockers twirling her hair. She really does look different this year.

"Are you going to go talk to her?"

"Now?"

"Yeah, come on Kevin we've only got a few months to live it up!"

"You're right, I'm out." And just like that Kevin walks right up to Nancy. I turn around looking for some of the other guys but see none, and then the bell rings so I just head straight to homeroom. I sit in one of the last seats and watch as everyone files into the room. All of a sudden I heard a laugh that I recognize oh to well. Jasmine walks in with some of her posy, and I say posy because the girl has no real friends, just a bunch of girls who want to be popular so they all try to get in her good gracious. I quickly turn my head so she won't see me. She walks one row over and heads towards the front of the room.

Jasmine and I, well, we were really "the it" couple. Both of us are popular and good looking. She has a petite body frame, gorgeous bright blue eyes, long wispy blond hair and she always wears bright red lip gloss. She's the caption of the cheerleading team and me the football. We had all the statistics going for us, but sadly that was it. I mean we were with each other, but there were no real connections or feelings. At least there were no real feelings after about the first 8 months. We cared for one another but never enough, we were just together. Right before prom last year we started having problems, somehow we got through that but on the last day of school, we broke up and it didn't end quietly or nicely for that matter. I don't have anything against Jasmine but she wasn't happy with me.

I glance back to the door and see Avery walk in by herself. I watch her sit down on the opposite side of the room. Before I have time to really think about what I'm doing, I find myself crossing the room in the back and stealing the seat behind her.

"Avery." She jumps at the sound of my voice and turns in her seat to face me.

"Michael, what are you doing?"

"I don't know, saying hi."

"I thought we agreed to end things."

"Does this mean I can't say hi?" She rolls her eyes at me but smiles.

"You realize how risky it is, we basically hate each other in school, and all of our classmates know that. Do you know how people will react if they see us together, and talking?" I know she's right. Everyone knows Avery and I never liked each other but truth be told, neither of us wanted the summer to end. But it did and now it's time to get over things, which is why I need to go back across the room.

"You're right."

"Like always." The bell rings and everyone in the room quiets down. I sit here not knowing what to do. The teacher makes it pretty easy for me because he starts doing roll call and before I know it, he's to my name.

"Michael Statemen."

I hesitate, "here"

"Michael!" all of a sudden Jasmine is looking at me, her eyes wide. "I didn't know you were in this homeroom! What are you doing over there? Don't you know the cool kids sit on this side of the room?" She sneers towards Avery. Oh boy, this is going to get ugly, but really though a senior using the word cool?

"Funny, I thought that was the side of the room people sat on if they have an STD." Avery shoots back.

"OOOOHHHH" everyone in the room says at the same time. That actually stung me considering Avery knows Jasmine and I were an item all of high school until now. And she knows that Jasmine and I never actually went all the way.

"Ouch." I say out loud. Told ya she could be bitchy. Avery looks and just stares. She won't give anything away and I don't know why I expect her too, we already stated that we agreed to end things.

"Ladies that is enough, Avery detention." Mr. Gage says. Avery gives a pissed off glance at Jasmine and if hell could freeze I'd swear it just did. I get up and walk across the room, taking the seat behind Jasmine. "So tell me all about your summer!" she gushes. I look one more time at Avery but she never looks back. What an awesome way to start the day.

By lunch all of us guys are together. It's Kevin, Joe, Lance, Parker, Shane, and myself. Joe's pretty much the rebel of the group, he doesn't care what anyone thinks about him, including the girls. He keeps his brown hair buzzed fairly short and all the girls just love to rub their hands through it, that's what he's known for. That and being a huge flirt. He's more muscle than anything else.

Lance is the pretty boy but doesn't know it. He's got short blond/brownish hair that he jells and blue eyes. Most girls swoon when he walks past, he either really doesn't get that they're into him, or he just doesn't care. He's the quiet one of the group, and probably the nicest of all of us.

Parker, well its Parker. He's cocky and funny at the same time. He's also the shortest of us guys, he's 5'9 and we never let him forget it. He's the guy that doesn't like to start conversations but he loves to comment on them. He's the one who either makes a smartass remark, or can lighten the mood when it gets too heavy.

Shane's a simple person who really just likes to be left alone. I mean he likes hanging out with all of us, but he usually keeps most things to himself. He looks almost exactly like Kevin, except with brown hair.

We are all of course excited and talking about our first game of the football season on Friday but we are even more excited with our plans for afterwards.

"I do believe I am going to ask Nancy if she would like to go with me." Kevin proclaims.

"Dude there is just something about her that freaks me out this year." Joe looks at Kevin, "So therefore I think you're stupid."

"It's a challenge bro, and she is gorgeous so I accept!"

"I don't think she's bad looking, maybe a little more aggressive." Parker throws in. "I saw her in chemistry pretty much thrusting herself at Caleb, her assigned lab partner."

"Don't care, still askin."

"What about you Shane?"

"Oh no, I'm not looking for any girl that's going to give me trouble or try to start any shit, I think I'm just going to lay low for a while." Last year Shane dated this girl who was something else. She faked a whole pregnancy ordeal to try to get Shane to marry her. Then when he tried to end it she acted suicidal, it wasn't pretty. Poor Shane went through everything to keep her happy. Her family moved which finally gave him the chance to end things, without him having to worry and see her every day. Apparently she started seeing this other guy right away so we don't think she was too heartbroken. I did feel bad for the other guy though, if only he knew.

"That's fair." We all sit there agreeing remembering and nodding our heads at the memories. I notice Lance looking around the cafeteria a lot.

"Alright Lance, your turn." I give him a look. "Who do you want to invite to the party?"

"Oh um, no one in particular just yet."

"You lie." We all laugh. We love giving Lance a hard time, he's always so serious and shy, but he's one of the sincerest and down to earth guys I've ever met. He looks at me. Oh boy, it's Jasmine. Lance and Jasmine together, hmm the thought is disturbing, and their personalities are way off. But then again I don't want her so if she makes him happy then more power to the both of them.

"Well you promise not to get mad Michael?"

"Whoever it is, I'm sure it's no big deal."

"I know you can't stand her, but today when we were talking I realized she's not bad at all and we get along on so many different levels, or at least I think we will. I mean we aren't anything yet by any means..." all of a sudden it hit me, hard "it's Avery Carson." Lance looks at me in a timid way.

"Why would I be upset about that?" The words came out tighter than I want.

"Well like I said you two have had your fair share of fights and I know you two don't like each other."

"No, it's cool man. You don't need my permission to date or like a girl." I take a drink of my water; this was not what I had expected at all, this was in fact weird. No one ever noticed Avery including myself, until this year and now two of us want her.

"You know she is cute, with the curls and slim figure and all" Parker remarks.

"Oh, you boys talking about me again?" Jasmine asks walking up and setting her trey down beside me.

"Always" Joe says. Jasmine throws her long hair over one shoulder and sits down. "So are you boys all ready and excited for Friday night's game?"

"When aren't we ready to play, especially since we're seniors?" Kevin the only besides Joe who's decent enough to respond, says.

"Yeah, but I'm really going to miss cheerleading when it's over."

"You still have all of basketball season, plus your competition season."

"I guess that's true." She picks up her fork and starts eating. We all are a bit thrown off as to why she's eating with us and not her friends. Hell we didn't even eat lunch together when we were dating. Lance gets up.

"Where are you going?" I know it's wrong to ask especially when I already know the answer but I'm curious to see if I'm right.

"To talk to Avery."

"Why her?" Jasmine sneers "She's ugly and bitchy and no one likes her. Why else do you think she is always by herself?"

"Because she's better than anyone and doesn't want to stoop down to their level of stupidity or YOUR level of fakeness" and with that Lance walks across the cafeteria while the other guys, including myself snicker. Most people don't talk back to Jasmine or talk smack, especially to her face, AND coming from Lance, that's awesome. I can't help but watch the whole time as he approaches Avery and they walk out the cafeteria doors together.

"So Michael, I want to talk to you." Jasmine says.

"Alright we're out, talk to you later man, we have to finish our details for Friday." Kevin gives me a high five as well as Shane, Parker and Joe and they all get up and leave. I haven't been alone with Jasmine since we broke up. I mean there was homeroom this morning but after I said my summer went well I zoned out to what she was saying. I think she was talking to her posy anyways.

"What?"

"Wow, someone is being mean. I thought when we broke up we agreed we would stay friends?"

"Actually you slapped me when we broke up, and I believe you threw punch in my face, said I was a dick and never deserved a girl as good as you." I give her a look. "So excuse me if sitting here and trying to be nice to you isn't working out so well."

"Okay, I get your point, but then again we've had the summer to both calm down and think about things. And I want to apologize. I never realized how great you were and I took advantage of you and for that I am truly sorry." I look into Jasmine's blue eyes and see sincerity for the first time in a long time. Part of me wants to take her in my arms and tell her everything is fine and that we could work this out, after all that's what's familiar to both of us. But at the same time the thought of holding her again makes my stomach turn. We were terrible together; I only wish I would have figured it out sooner. It seems funny that I had spent so much time with Jasmine but I never felt anything when we broke up. I didn't feel like my whole world fell apart, maybe because it had already been torn apart with Max passing and all. I only felt an emptiness but as soon as I met Avery that was gone.

"I believe you." A sweet smile sweeps across her face.

"I know you may not think that I'm changing but I am, and I want to prove it to you."

"I don't think that's such a good idea."

"Come on Michael, we dated for two in a half years and yes we threw it away but I want it back. I'm willing to change and go the extra mile to prove that to you. I changed over the summer, let me show you. Just give me a chance."

"It's the first day of school Jasmine, let's just take things slow, it's not like we have to rush into anything. And I'm not even sure if I want to." She looks pissed.

"You and your always needing time. You're almost as bad as an indecisive teenage girl. What happened to that rush of love we felt back freshman year? You know when you couldn't take your eyes off me, or keep your hands off either. I mean come on, you asked me out on the second day of school." Every word is dripping with attitude and sass. And just like that the real Jasmine is back. "Sorry, habit, anyways I want to spend time with you this weekend, so text me." She gets up and leaves. As I watch her go I feel a ping for what we use to have. I could have her back, the question is do I want her back. I sit here for a second feeling confused. Maybe it's because being together is what's normal for us.

Then for some reason I think about the day my family found out my brother died. I remember crying like a baby and when I told Jasmine, she put her arms around me and said "Sweetie all good things must come to an end eventually, some sooner than others." We sat there like that for ten minutes then she looked at me and said "are you going to be sad forever because you're really bringing me down and Stacey's having a party tonight." No I certainly did not want that back. The only reason Jasmine wants to be with me is because I'm technically the most popular guy and she's the most popular girl. Well that isn't good enough for me. I want someone who can be my best friend, not saying that I have to find her now, I mean hell, I've still got all of college, but I know that girl is definitely not Jasmine.

Chapter Two

After practice on my way home I think about sneaking over to Avery's. I know that sounds bad but I want to talk to her. I want in all honesty to tell her not to go out with Lance. But I can't, Lance is my friend, he's always supported me and I want him to feel like he can count on me to support him. More than anything I'm mad at myself. If I like Avery then why can't I just admit it, but there's something holding me back, I'm just not sure what it is yet. Hell maybe I actually do like being single. I mean I don't have to worry about pleasing anybody else; I can do whatever I want when I want.

I pull into my driveway and get out. I want to shower and enjoy an evening off of work, however I notice Whinny walking over.

"Uh, Hey Michael." She rubs her arm and looks at me in a timid way.

"Whinny." She actually lives next door to me and is in my class. She's on the cheerleading team with Jasmine; she's a flyer and the only person in the school who does one on one partner stunting with Jimmy Aswell, which is apparently why they've won state all three years of us being in high school. At least that's what Jasmine always said, "no other high school has a couple that does partner stunting, usually everything is done with a build. It makes us that much greater."

Jimmy's the only guy on the cheerleading team. A lot of people gave him a pretty hard time at first but once they saw the things he and Whinny could do, they shut up pretty fast. Plus, he always brags about getting to be around girls in sports bras and short shorts. None of us could argue with that.

Whinny never really says much, so it's hard to picture her being on the cheerleading squad. We've never really talked before at least not since we were kids. I mean occasionally we'll share a glance or a wave but otherwise we've just pretended we don't exist to each other. I'm not sure why but that's just the way it's been since we were kids. When we were young we use to play together, her, me and my brother, but once my brother grew up and told me she had cooties I ignored her, we both did.

Her brown kinky hair falls about mid back but is currently piled on top of her head. She has on a blue tank top and white shorts. She's also wearing glasses. It's the first time I've ever really looked at her. I mean I've glanced every now and then, she's the hot next door neighbor girl who wouldn't? But this is the first time I've ever been this close to her at least since she's hit puberty. She has green eyes and her face is unreadable. I realize she's tiny, probably even smaller than Jasmine, she's tan and smells like strawberries and peaches.

"Look, I'm sorry to bother you, but my kitten is stuck up in our Oak tree in the back yard. I tried getting him down myself, but I ended up falling. He's still stuck, and I'd rather not break a bone, do you think you could get him?"

"Sure, just let me go get a ladder and I'll be right over."

"Thanks so much." She turns and starts towards her side of the fence. I notice her right elbow is scratched pretty badly and coated with dried blood, must have been a tough fall.

I trek on inside and notice mom left a note saying she was working overtime again. She started doing this all of July, not coming home until seven or eight. Bless her; she's got to be the best mother around. I know she's doing all of this for me. She wants us to be well off, but I don't expect her to be working this much or this hard. I leave the note and head towards the back yard where I retrieve the ladder out of our tool barn and head back over to Whinny's.

"Wow he got himself stuck way up there."

"Yeah."

"So how far up where you when you fell?"

She blushes "the limb right under him. I stood up to reach for him and down I went."

"Well damn that's like a seven-foot drop, while dodging branches too." I look at her but she's looking elsewhere. I notice that she's beautiful. Breath taking is probably a better word, she isn't wearing any make-up, and just looks pure. Her skin looks soft and smooth, I mean not that I've felt it, just based off looks.

There's something about her that calms me, I can feel it now, all the stress from the first day of senior year and of practice is just gone for the moment. I feel relaxed. She looks at me and our eyes lock for a split second before I look away feeling embarrassed for starring. My heart is practically beating out of my chest which seems weird since I feel calm.

"So you think you can get MD?"

"Medical Doctor?"

"Milk Dud" She smiles a small smile. "Impressive guess though."

"I'm smarter than you'd think. Creative name though" She pushes her glasses up on her nose.

"Thanks" I set the ladder up and climb up it. I notice Whinny moves and takes hold of the ladder to keep it balanced. It takes me by surprise, but maybe that's because I'm used to having to ask Jasmine to do something for me. Not that the ladder really needs to be held, I'm on flat ground but the thought is what counts. I start calling the kitten's name. It sure is a friendly thing, as soon as I get to a point where I can put my hand out, he crawls right in meowing and purring the whole time. The rescue is rather easy. I descend down the ladder and safely hand the little guy back over to Whinny.

"Thanks Michael. I really appreciate it."

"No problem. You know he's kind of cute." I pet the grey and white fluff ball sitting in her hands.

"He's a good cuddle partner."

"Well everyone needs one of those." I smile and gather up the ladder.

"I better go." She smiles at me then turns and heads to her house. It looks pretty empty.

"Are your parent's home?" I'm not sure why I ask, it just kind of came out. She slowly turns back towards me.

"No, they're out of town."

"You want to come over, order a pizza and watch a movie?" I have no idea what I'm doing. We've never hung out before, literally this is the first time we've spent more than thirty seconds around each other, this could be awkward as hell, but for some reason after taking another look at her arm I have this weird feeling. I feel I guess protective of her. I can't explain it. I know I'm going to be alone tonight but I don't want her to be.

Besides I could use some girl advice about the whole Avery thing, and asking Whinny doesn't seem like a bad idea.

"You want to spend time with me? We've never hung out before Michael. Not since what, when we were six? I mean thanks for asking but…"

"What are you afraid of?" I cut her off. In my head I'm screaming 'what are you doing? Stop talking' but that's not what's coming out of my mouth. For some reason I didn't quite like hearing her say no.

"That we might actually have a few things in common and become friends and have fun." I put my hand to my mouth making a cheesy gasp sign. She smirks.

"Are you challenging me to come over and hang out with you?"

I think for a minute. "What answer will get you to come?"

She laughs "alright I'll come, let me put MD back and clean up my arm."

"There ya go! See you in a few." I take the ladder back and head inside to take a quick shower. For some reason I'm not feeling so exhausted anymore. I'm actually feeling excited. I shake out my hair, put on shorts and a football sectional champion shirt from freshmen year and head back downstairs just as Whinny is approaching the back porch.

"Okay, I'm starved, so what type of pizza would you like?" I waste no time jumping into the food conversation. I'm actually really nervous too, I know I shouldn't be, it's not like this is a date or anything. It's just this will be the only other girl I've spent any one on one time with besides Jasmine and Avery.

"Guess being a hard working athlete will do that to you." Her voice is actually very soothing.

"Football practices have been rough this year. But hey you're a cheerleader, so don't tell me you don't work up an appetite." Although I'll admit it doesn't look like she eats anything. I'm guessing she weighs 100 pounds if that. She doesn't look sickly though, she looks lean and muscular.

"No I do. Any kind of pizza, but I especially love mushrooms." I look at her for the first time since she came back over, she's smiling and for some reason it makes me smile and it relaxes me.

"How about Mushroom, pepperoni, and cheese?"

"Sounds good." I walk into my mom and dad's bedroom located off the kitchen to make the call. After I get off the phone I stand in the room a minute. Am I aware of what I'm doing? I mean Whinny is in my house for crying out loud. And I wanted her to come. I have a feeling this night is going to be long. I have no idea what I just got myself in to.

I take a deep breath and walk back out. I wonder what in the hell the two of us are going to talk about, but then I notice Whinny looking at our family pictures, in an instant everything I was just feeling in the bedroom disappears. There's something about her presence, it makes me feel in a weird way I guess safe. Maybe it's the way she's looking at the photos that eases me. I know she won't judge me; I'm just getting this vibe. I feel some of my walls come down. I feel like telling her about my brother and how close we actually were. I feel like telling her how I feel about my family. But I don't dare go into that conversation; to me it's the most personal thing about me.

To be honest it didn't help that Max passing was the only reason my dad reenlisted in the military. He couldn't take being here so he left mom and me when we were at our lowest. And for that part alone I'll never be able to forgive him. I love him and still talk to him, when I get a chance but there will be some part of me that will forever be scarred. I take things a lot more personally then probably necessary. The death of Max and dad leaving really has changed me.

I stand and just watch her. She has no idea I'm back. I can tell she's really looking at the pictures. The pictures of family vacations, and our send off to Max before he went overseas. I feel like by just looking at those she can read me. I swallow a lump in my throat.

"See any you like?" I finally say making her jump a little.

"All of them." She says turning around. "My mom hates having her picture taken. We don't have any family photos."

"My mom doesn't like it either, but she loves taking the pictures and capturing memories."

Whinny smiles she can tell something struck a nerve with me. "Be thankful. To me every picture can have a five-minute story behind it. Plus, it's fun to look back and see how much you've grown and changed over the years."

"I am, for everything. Life has its ups and downs, but I'm here." We stand staring at each other. I feel very vulnerable. I know she's reading me and there's nothing I can do about it.

"You don't have a single picture of yourself when you were young?"

She looks sad "nope, not one." I want to look away but I can't leave her green eyes. They're pulling me in and making me want to stay. In a silent way it's like she's talking to me telling me everything will be fine.

My phone goes off, insinuating I have a text. It pulls us from our intense stare off moment. I pull my phone out of my shorts pocket. It's from Jasmine. I just stare at it.

"She'd freak if she knew I was here."

I look Whinny dead in the eyes with a smirk on my face. "How'd you know who this is?"

She shrugs her shoulders "Jasmine hasn't stopped talking about you all summer. And no offense but what Jasmine wants, Jasmine gets."

"Oh really?"

"Come on Michael. You babied her and you know it. She's spoiled, that girl has never had to work for anything a day in her life." Now I can tell I've struck a nerve with Whinny. I have a feeling Whinny has a terrible opinion of the type of person I am. I bet Jasmine has been going around telling stories that aren't true and that's an uneasy thought and feeling.

"Well it doesn't matter this time, I don't care about her anymore at least not in the 'I want to date you and spend every single moment with you' way. We treated each other like crap. Getting out of that relationship was the best thing for us." I don't reply back to the text.

"Don't you mean she treated you like crap? The whole school knows basically the ins and outs of you and Jasmine."

"Oh." The wonderful perks of going to a small school. I wonder how much of what the whole school knows are actually true things that happened between us? I want to ask Whinny some stories she's heard, but at the same time I really don't want to talk about Jasmine.

"You're a good guy Michael; and so you spoiled her, but you don't have to drag yourself down with her." She smiles then heads into our living room. I follow and head over to our movie case and start pulling some movies out. I guess this conversation is closed.

"So what movie sounds like it would spark your interest?" I ask Whinny.

"Something funny" She falls into our couch and it surprises me how she looks like she fit in with everything. She looks happy and comfortable. The only girl I've had over here has been Jasmine. However, she complained that our house was too small so we spent the majority of our time at her place.

"How about *THE HANGOVER?*"

"Perfect." The door chimes while I'm setting up the movie. She gets up, answers the door, pays the pizza guy and comes back to the couch.

"Are we allowed to eat in here?"

"Yes, why did you pay for that?"

"It's no biggie. Besides you saved my kitty." She makes a funny face after she says kitty, then corrects herself "kitten."

I go in the kitchen and get us drinks. We sit on opposite ends of the couch with the pizza box in between us. By the time the movie is halfway through it feels like we're old friends just hanging out, each of us making comments as the movie plays and we laugh. We both laugh out loud. I can tell she's relaxed and just enjoying herself. I can tell I'm actually relaxed too, for once I'm not really thinking about anything except her. When the movie is actually over and the credits are rolling I feel depressed, for some stupid reason I don't want her to go.

"Thanks for asking me to come over for a while. It's nice to be invited places."

"You never getting invited anywhere? Come on get real. I'm pretty sure you're going to win class congeniality. Everyone loves you." Which is true, I've never really seen Whinny around school, but everyone always talks about her and how nice she is. I guess she talks to almost everyone in our school. She's just a really nice girl to everybody she meets.

"There's a difference between being nice to people and people liking you. Just because I'm nice doesn't necessarily mean someone likes me. But for the record I'm not worried about our senior personality things. I'm not out to impress people, I'm out to live my life. And I don't get invited places because I'm just usually swamped working so therefore people stop asking me if I want to do things when my response is always no."

She has a valid point. "I still can't believe you don't get invited places. And I know for a fact over half the school does actually like you."

"Well thanks for that load of confidence." She says sarcastically. I laugh. "And I'm used to it I've been working since I was allowed; I think I had my first job when I was thirteen."

"Why?" She shrugs her shoulders and I can tell she doesn't want to talk about it anymore so I switch the subject.

"Why don't you wear contacts?"

"I do at school and what not, but at night after I wash my face and am basically ready for bed I have to take them out."

"You mean to tell me you were ready for bed at six today?"

"No, I just got out of the shower and didn't want to put contacts back in. But I was planning on being in bed early since I had little homework to do."

"Oh come on!"

She laughs "you don't understand my life. This is the first night I've had off in two months."

"Not even any weekends?"

"No. I work two jobs sometimes three; it's always go go go."

"Plus cheerleading?"

"Plus cheerleading, it's kind of my life right now." She turns and faces me. "You know you sure are asking a lot of questions."

"I'm sorry. You're turn, ask me anything." Right then my mom comes walking in carrying groceries with her.

"Hey Michael, and Whin Whinny?" She looks baffled; mom knows that my brother and I haven't had anything to do with Whinny in a while.

"Hello Mrs. Statemen, do you need help?"

"Oh no, but thanks for asking."

"Mom let us help." I get up and Whinny follows me out to my mom's jeep liberty.

"That was really nice of you to offer and help. Thank you." She shrugs her shoulders.

"Mothers are heroes in disguise; it's nice to be their sidekick." She takes some bags and walks inside. I smile. What an interesting thing to say.

Once everything is unloaded Whinny says she needs to go.

"I'll walk you."

"It's literally across the yard."

"It's dark out and the principal of the thing." So I count and take about twenty steps with Whinny from my front door to hers.

"Thanks for saving MD, the movie and pizza." She smiles and unlocks her door.

"Actually you paid for the pizza, which I feel bad about. I wish you'd let me repay you, but you're welcome and thank you for coming."

"I'm stubborn."

"Oh joy." She smiles. She has a very pretty smile. "I think for not talking to each other in years that went pretty well."

"Were you expecting less? Or More?"

"I wasn't expecting anything but some good company." She nods her head.

"Well goodnight Whinny." I start to walk away.

"Hey Michael"

"Yeah" I turn back towards her.

"I never told you this and I'm sorry if now is an inappropriate time, but I am very sorry for you losing your brother. I know how close you two were. No one should have to go through that." I don't say anything for a moment. She's talking about my most sensitive subject. She can tell too.

"Thanks Whinny." She goes inside, and I finish the steps I have left back home. I walk in the door ready for bed but the way mom is looking at me means it might be a while yet.

"Yes?"

"I like her." Mom wasn't a fan of Jasmine; I think she jumped for joy when we broke up.

"Mom"

"Why was she here?" I'm about to respond when I realize I never asked Whinny what she thought I should do about Avery, in fact I had forgotten about Avery all together. I finally pull my phone out of my pocket, after Jasmine's text I had put it on silent. Three texts from Avery and another one from Jasmine. Opps.

"Her kitten was stuck in the tree and I helped her get him down, then for some reason I asked her over here, I guess for some stupid reason I was feeling lonely and the thought of company didn't sound too bad."

"There's nothing wrong with that."

"I'm a guy mom, we don't get lonely."

"Everyone gets lonely some time or another Michael." Moms face falls slightly.

"I really wanted her opinion on something, you know girl advice, but when she was over here I completely forgot."

"Well" mom pauses and I know she's going to launch into a mother speech. "She's very polite which always rates high in my book. It just surprised me since you and your brother acted like she was the plague."

Not what I was expecting. "Yeah, we were idiots." The thought of having ignored Whinny for the past ten years upsets me.

"I guess you're growing up after all." Mom smiles and I roll my eyes, but it was probably true. I guess I thought I was invincible, until my brother.

"Anything I can help you with? I am a woman after all."

I think for a second. What the hell, mom may not have a clue what I'm talking about but I guess it couldn't hurt to ask. "Do you think if you used to get into arguments with someone of the opposite sex and everyone knew you two couldn't stand each other, but then one day you realized they aren't as bad as you once thought, do you think you should go for it? I mean let's say you've kind of been seeing each other but haven't told anyone, do you think you should let everyone else in?"

"It depends."

"Well this was a great chat." Mom laughs.

"I guess it could work. As long as when you're together you aren't always butting heads. You'll never know unless you try. As long as you feel like the feelings are there, that she's not just filling a gap or that you just want to be with her to prove everyone wrong. And trust me, as a word of advice it helps to have a few things in common. That way you can go out and enjoy activities together." Mom puts the milk in the fridge. "I'm guessing you aren't talking about Whinny."

"You're going to try and push her on me now aren't you?"

"No, no, it's your life. I would never do that. I never pushed you to end things with Jasmine even when I didn't like her. I'm just saying that for the whole two minutes I was here, she seemed like a sweetheart. She grew up well." I give mom a look.

"Yeah, well she's probably going to win the girls side of class congeniality, She's nice to everyone mom, so don't feel too special."

"Ha ha."

"Goodnight."

"Night, sweetie." As I head up the stairs I wonder if what mom said is what's holding me back with Avery. Maybe it really is that I like being single and the only reason I want to be with her is because now someone else wants her. Maybe she's right about wanting to prove people wrong. I guess that talk helped, or did it really just confuse me more? I also think about how sincere Whinny was. Mom's right, she did grow up well.

Chapter Three

The next day during homeroom I notice Avery looking at me. When I turn and fully look at her, she mouths something. I figure it would be easier to text her. As soon as I get out my phone the teacher walks in.

"Detention Michael"

"Oh come on."

"Shouldn't have gotten your phone out" Mr. Gage says. Hope mom doesn't find out about this, she'll be all over me.

After homeroom I stall so Avery and I are walking out the door at the same time.

"You get detention yesterday; I get it today." I say.

"Pity, anyways come over tonight at around nine-thirty." I look at her, and she nods.

"Alright" We quickly separate. I'm not sure exactly what I'm feeling or thinking. She and Lance looked pretty chummy yesterday. I can't hurt him, bros before hoes. As I walk down the hall to my locker Jasmine grabs my arm.

"You didn't text me back." She pouts

"You texted me?"

"Last night."

"My phone was dead."

"Well Michael, if we are going to make this work."

"We aren't" I cut her off and she looks baffled. I don't usually stand up for myself. That's why everyone was in shock when they found out I was actually the one who ended our relationship in the first place. Jasmine wanted everyone to think she was the one who wanted it to be over.

"Excuse me?"

"You were talking about that rush of love yesterday, and guess what, it's gone. It was gone long ago Jas and it's time for both of us to just move on." I walk past her leaving her with her mouth hanging open. Probably won't be the last time I see her today.

I can't concentrate in any of my morning classes. I'm upset that I have detention and all because I was going to send Avery a text. My first detention ever and it's over this girl? Seriously. Then I also happen to find myself thinking about Whinny. In between periods today I've tried looking for her but I haven't seen her. Our school and our class isn't that big. Finally, the bell rings and I'm free to head to lunch.

At lunch all us guys are again talking about who we want to invite to the after party on Friday. Lance is dead set on asking Avery. He talks so highly of her. Apparently they have Chemistry two together, and I guess study hall. Must be some chemistry making going on in Chemistry.

"She and I we just have a connection. We can talk about anything."

"Awe someone's getting all deep and attached. You better slow down there bud, it's the second day of senior year, and you don't want to end up like our good friend Michael. Don't be whipped already." Parker teases.

"Shut up man." Lance and I say at the same time. We all talk some more. So far Parker and Shane are going solo. Kevin had already asked Nancy and she said she wanted nothing more than to go to a party with him. Joe said he was going to ask Melanie but strictly as friends, he's too cool to be tied down to just one girl for right now. As for me, well I'm not sure if I want to ask anyone. Part of me wants to ask Whinny just as friends but at the same time I have these weird feelings for Avery. We had a great summer together talking, that's just it, we only talked. I remember what mom said about having common interests and doing things, I'm not sure if Avery and I have that. Hell I'm not sure what's going on between us or even if there is an us. I'm excited to see what she wants to talk to me about tonight. It's either going to be good, or bad. Then again I feel horrible sneaking over to see her, when Lance feels the way he does about her. If it's the same feelings I had once for Jasmine, then I know he's in deep.

After school I head to the detention room passing a bunch of gothic kids and Avery who's with them. They all have piercings and tattoos and are decked out in black. I glance at her as a guy throws his arm around her shoulders.

"Bruce get off." She yanks his hand away.

"Come on Avery, you liked me last year." He throws his arm around her again.

"Hey." I call, I stop walking after they've passed and turn back towards them. "Give the girl some respect." The guy narrows his eyes at me.

"What are you going to do about it tough guy?"

"Oh my gosh Bruce get over yourself." Avery says and starts walking away again. He glares at me.

"You're lucky she walked away, didn't want to have to hurt your pretty face in front on her."

I turn back around and keep walking to the detention room. As I walk further away from Avery I keep hoping I'll feel that feeling of wanting to protect her. I mean I never want to see a girl be abused by a guy, but I'm just not sure I'm having those feelings, I don't have that same overacted feeling I got when I saw Whinny's arm.

As I walk into the detention room I think about how much I'm going to hate being half an hour late to practice. I wonder how much coach is going to punish me. I take a seat in the second row in the third last seat. I finally notice I'm the only one. Must be because it's only the second day of school, usually teachers don't start giving out detentions until two months in. The teacher, Miss Dawson walks in.

"First time I think I've ever seen you here."

"I've decided to become a rebel."

She laughs "Oh no, guess we all better watch out for you."

"Nah, the only place you have to watch out for me, is on the football field."

"I hear you guys are supposed to be really good this year. The best looking team we've had in about four years. Apparently word on the street is you've practiced all summer, even doing three a day. I'm excited for Friday's game."

"Yeah we did it was pretty intense and I think we all are."

"I wonder why this year coach decided to push you all so hard."

"Because he knew we would be the team that could handle it. Plus, there are a lot of great guys coming up and he's working on molding them into a winning program." She laughs again and bats her eyes. She's sitting on the edge of her desk with her legs crossed and wearing a short skirt, trust me, I noticed. She's young, I think this is only her second year here, she came straight from college. She has short thin blond hair but for some reason she does absolutely nothing for me. Every other guy in this school thinks she's drop dead gorgeous, and is constantly trying to flirt with her. Don't get me wrong she's pretty, but sitting here being able to make her laugh so easily and knowing she's slightly flirting with me, does nothing for me.

"Alright well I'm supposed to detain you." I nod my head and look at the clock. It's 3:10, only twenty more minutes of silence thanks to Miss Dawson for killing ten. I find myself thinking about Whinny again. I'm not sure why. I mean two days ago if I was in this same situation and you asked me who I would be thinking about, it would have been Avery. But I haven't seen Whinny all day. I just have a funny feeling that something isn't right. I don't know what it is.

"You're free to go Michael." I look up at the clock.

"Wow those twenty minutes flew by."

"You must have some pretty important stuff on your mind then."

"Yeah, I guess."

"Don't get into trouble again, and good luck Friday. I'm hoping I won't see you before then." She smiles real big.

"You won't and thanks." I run all the way to the football field's locker room, change faster than I ever have before and run out to the field.

Coach made me run a lot for being late, he also made me do some hardcore ab routines for twenty minute intervals with four breaks, but I was okay with it. As quarterback I feel I should be the most in shape. The practice went really well, all of our defensive guys were actually able to run the full length of the football field and back without stopping, at a pretty quick pace. Offense spent most of the practice running the bleachers, then catching. I had to do the bleachers with the offense and run the field with the defense, plus throwing for my wide receivers, and tight end, namely Kevin, Chris and sometimes Lance. Lance is usually my main running back, but this year coach has wanted him to practice catching so we can work on lateral plays. I definitely think we'll be ready for Friday. All the guys on the team want this season to be the best, especially us seniors, we want more than to just be sectional champions this year.

Once in my truck and on the way home I call work and ask if I could have off since I had to stay later at practice than everyone. I told them I could work double on Saturday so they let it slide. I pull in the driveway and look at Whinny's house. It looks dead again. I just sit and watch for ten minutes but nothing happens. I wonder when her parents are going to get back home.

Finally, I get out and head inside. It's going on seven and I'm starving. Mom isn't home yet; I'm starting to think this is going to become a typical thing. She used to get off around four and would be home by four thirty.

I want to wait and eat with her so I decide taking a shower should be the first thing in order. When I come back down stairs mom's home, however she looks as pale as a ghost.

"Mom what's wrong?" I instantly think of my dad being overseas.

"Nothing."

"Are you okay?"

"I'm fine; I need to take a drive."

"Is dad okay?"

"Yes."

"You just got home; you don't need to go anywhere. You need to tell me what's wrong." I walk over and take her arm. She's shaking.

"Everything's fine." She snaps, jerking away from me. She starts walking for the front door. I step in front of her.

"Mom, what the hell is going on? You're scaring me."

"Let go Michael." She pushes me out of the way and I grab her arm again. She turns with her other hand and slaps me across the face.

"Oh, my Gosh." She starts crying even more and runs to her car. I'm startled by the slap.

"Mom!" I finally yell after regaining my bearings. I call after her standing in the doorway. I watch as she pulls away. I feel speechless. Mom has never hit anyone before and granite it was just a slap, it was very unexpected and very unlike our family. I've seen mom break down before but this doesn't seem like a breakdown. It seems like she's mortified, scared, committed a murder, hell I don't know. This isn't a regular break down, this is intense. My head is spinning with confusion I need something to take my mind off things. I need someone to talk to.

Without realizing what I'm doing I find myself standing on Whinny's front porch, even though the house still looks dead. I knock anyways and to my surprise Whinny actually opens the door. She has an ice pack in her hand and a black and blue left eye.

"What the hell?"

"It's nothing." Without thinking I take my hands and cup her face, turning her head so I can see her eye. Her skin is as soft and smooth as it looks. I feel an intense spark run through my body. She looks so innocent and fragile here in this moment, however I know she's not, or at least she doesn't want anyone to think she is.

"It's nothing? Whinny your eye is almost swollen shut" I turn her head back so I'm looking dead into her green eyes, well one green eye, the other is pretty swollen. She doesn't budge. "Who did this to you?"

"Michael" she pushes my hands away "you don't have to look after me, it's not your job and you're not my boyfriend." She's right. I have no idea why I want to protect her so badly. Then I think back to how I had a weird feeling something with her wasn't right today.

"That doesn't mean I don't care." I bite my tongue; did I really just say that out loud?

"Ha care? Are you serious? You've never talked or had anything to do with me in years until yesterday, a whopping 24 hours, and now you care?" She's agitated probably a little more than agitated. She actually looks like she might cry.

I breathe out. "Yes, and I know it sounds crazy and I wish I could explain myself but I can't. I just don't want to see anything hurt you. I feel like you're a person who's always happy and full of life and I don't want to see anyone or anything take that away from you."

And then just like that a tear does fall. "Don't Michael, just don't." She slams the door on me. I stand here a moment trying to take things in. Mom was all freaked out and Whinny has a black eye and slammed the door on me. Am I sensing this could be related? Hell, I'm striking out on talking to girls; my night is starting out terrible, no this whole day had started off terrible.

I go back home and make myself a sandwich. Before anything else happens tonight I need food. While eating I watch some T.V. hoping it will distract me. It's a fail. I want to talk to Whinny again and I want to talk to mom, but at the moment it didn't look like either was going to happen.

At nine mom still isn't home. I'm beginning to worry. She's been gone for two hours; I give her cell phone a call, the counter top starts ringing. Go figure she left her phone here at home. This night is going wrong and I need to fix it. So I take twenty paces back over to Whinny's. She opens the door again.

"Sorry I slammed the door in your face."

"I guess I deserved it."

"You were just trying to be a good friend. I mean friends look out for each other." For some reason I don't like the sound of good friend.

"I guess I just don't want to see you hurt. I mean you already took quite a fall from the tree."

"I'm a big girl, I can handle myself. I've never needed anyone to look after me before and I don't need it now." The bite in her voice stings a little. I know I shouldn't be pushing her buttons, especially since we just started talking for the first time in years.

"Okay." We don't say anything for a minute, so I break the silence. "So are your parent's home?" I'm bringing up anything I can just to keep this conversation going and to try and turn it around. I hate this feeling I'm having, the feeling of her being mad at me.

"Not until Saturday."

"Wow you have the house to yourself all week. Can I come in?" My phone goes off. I quickly look at it, hoping it's from mom using someone else's phone letting me know she's okay. Instead it's a text from Avery. I forgot about meeting her tonight, she's telling me I should come over now. I look up and can tell Whinny is able to read my face. I'm not use to that.

"I bet you have better things to do. I'm tired anyways." I feel even worse all of a sudden.

"Did you have to work tonight?"

"Yes. Michael, just go."

"Whinny, I can't walk away knowing you're mad at me."

"Because you care?" She says sarcastically.

I nod my head at her. "Michael it's fine, we're fine, we'll still be friends."

I hesitate "alright, but I still want to know who did this to you and when I find out, I'm getting even." I know she's upset with me.

"Okay tough guy."

"Oh one question though." She stops closing the door.

"Go ahead."

"You haven't seen or heard from my mom have you? She looked terrible tonight and she took off without talking to me. I'm worried something's desperately wrong."

"Nope, haven't seen or heard anything. Night" she closes the door in a hurry, but lightly this time. Then she opens it again. "But I'm sure everything is perfectly fine with your mom." The door closes again.

I smile. I feel so confused. I've only talked to Whinny for two days, and I'm not even sure if today would really count, but I feel as if I never want to leave. I feel like it's everything I have to walk away from her. I want to hold her until her black eye heals and I want to beat the crap out of the person who did this to her.

However, at the same time I'm feeling more than excited to see Avery. I'm hoping we will talk forever like we normally do. I'm missing her. Is it possible that I have fallen for two girls? But how when they're complete opposites?

I go back home and leave a short note for mom telling her I needed some air so I took a walk, then walk the four blocks to Avery's, go around back and tap on her bedroom window. She climbs out, jumps in my arms, and kisses my neck.

"I've missed you." She says as I set her down.

"Really, because you and Lance seem to be getting along pretty well."

"I think we are which scares me, because I want you."

We climb up to the top of the hill in the back of Avery's yard and lay looking up at the stars.

"You're quiet, what's going on?" she asks.

"Nothing" For some reason I don't feel like talking about my mom with Avery. Actually I don't really feel like talking about anything.

"Well didn't you hear what I said? I like Lance, I really do, but I feel like there's so much more here with you and me. I don't want to lose what we have." I roll on my side and look at her.

"Lance is one of my best guys."

"So you're saying you don't want to hurt him, I understand that." I take her hand.

"Do you honestly think we could ever be anything more than just sneaking away a few hours a day to be with each other?" She looks at me. "I mean maybe we both just like the thrill of knowing that in the school world we hate each other, but outside of school we have something but we have to be sneaky about it."

"Michael." She takes her hand back. "Are you saying that we never cared for each other?"

"I'm saying maybe we both liked the idea of being together just because it was thrilling to keep our relationship hidden." She looks hurt. I can't believe what I'm saying. Am I really breaking things off with her? But didn't we already technically break things off when school started?

"I shouldn't have asked you to come over here. I should have just left things alone. I guess I just thought you might have wanted to see me as much as I wanted to see you."

"I did. I missed you."

"Then why are you saying all of this?"

"If you really miss me as much as you say you do then you wouldn't be with Lance. You wouldn't keep leading him on. He really likes you and I know the feelings he has and their hardcore."

"He's a great companion."

"He's a human with feelings and you don't hear the way he talks about you."

"I'm lonely Michael, he takes that loneliness away." I think about what she said, and then I wonder if that was how I was feeling with Whinny. Maybe I was lonelier than I thought and she was there to keep me occupied.

She talks again. "I want you, and if you ever feel like you can give up your macho manor to be with me in public then I'll be waiting. I promised Lance I'd go to that stupid party with him Friday, but after that I'll break things off. I really don't care what other people think anymore. We like each other and no one should stop us. This isn't Romeo and Juliet's era we're living in." She has tears in her eyes. I lean in and kiss her.

By ten thirty I'm home again, thinking about the events that had occurred this evening. I peek in moms' room and she's sleeping. I head upstairs and jump in my own bed. Avery admitted to actually wanting to be with me, she didn't care anymore, so why should I? I know I like her a lot, but I guess I'm not sure if I want to actually be her boyfriend. Maybe I don't want to be with anyone. When Jasmine and I started dating I wanted to be with her all the time, football practice and her cheerleading practices were the only things standing in our way. But with Avery if I happen to be busy during the day and can't see her until that night, or couldn't see her at all, I don't mind. And I know I don't have those same intense feelings I had when Jas and I first started dating. It's a different kind of feeling I have for her, but still I feel like this should be a sign.

Then I think about Whinny. She's relaxed and I like that. I find myself wanting to talk to her even now. I also find myself wanting to protect her; I've never felt like that with Jasmine or Avery. I have no idea what is going on and why she keeps popping into my mind. But I actually like her being there. The thought of her comforts me and it makes me smile thinking of the next time I'll get to see her again.

Chapter Four

It's finally Friday and everyone is hyped up about the game. And I guess you could say everyone is pretty excited for the party that is supposed to occur after the game. We senior boys on the football team have somehow managed to have a party on top of the school roof. Which is actually pretty idiotic of us considering we could get in a crap ton of trouble. But we also said we were going to leave behind a legacy, and this is just one of the ways we're showing it.

The morning has flown by and now sitting here at lunch with all the guys just seems to make things worse on the nerves. I'm excited for tonight, first game of our senior year. The season has a lot riding on it. Everyone is throwing comments around and acting like crazy freshmen. I'm sitting back taking it all in. I'm not about to act like a kid who had way too much sugar.

"I'm going to ask her out tonight." Lance leans over and tells me. He's just sitting back watching the others as well.

"Really?"

"Yeah, the past two days she's been kind of distant and I think it's because she wants more. I know school's just started but I feel it's what both of us want. I need to get her close to me again." I feel so bad for him. I went over to Avery's Tuesday and Wednesday night. I know deep down she's waiting on me to make my move. That's just it, she wants commitment, Lance is right on that part. How could I do this to him? He's one of my best guys, plus he really likes her and to be honest I don't know if I do. We had a great summer no doubt but we never really did anything. We made out a lot, I think more than anything we have a strong physical attraction for one another. I'm not sure there's anything more. Maybe we do actually need to test the waters and see if a relationship could work. For some reason the two nights that I was over there I felt like we were growing apart, Lance just said the same thing. Huh, but then again I guess we've never really been together.

"Good for you. I hope she says yes."

"Do you really?" I look at him. "Or are you going to sneak over to her place after the party and tell her not to? I know you're the reason why she's been distant Michael." I'm stunned.

"What?"

"I think you know what I said."

"Lance." I'm confused. "I don't know what she's been telling you."

"I'm just disappointed you didn't." He gets up and gives me a look before saying "Let's have a good game tonight ladies" all the guys' whoop and holler as Lance walks off. I look towards Avery; she's staring at me. I get up. I want answers, how dare she think she can come between us. I know I'm not helping the situation but Lance and I have been friends since first grade and if anyone is going to screw it up, it would be him or me, although I guess he kind of knows that it's me.

I start walking across the cafeteria when I see Whinny for the first time since Tuesday. She's sitting with the other cheerleaders, all of them dressed in their uniforms. The uniforms every guy in this school loves because their mid drift tops and of course the skirts are short. And lucky for us we get to see them wear 'em ninety percent of the time. The cheerleaders usually wear their uniforms anytime there's a sporting event taking place. So basically everyday but Wednesday.

Whinny's black eye is looking much better, all the swelling is gone, but it's pretty colorful. There's no amount of makeup in the world that could cover it. I want her to notice me. I want her smile to be directed towards me. But she never turns her head, so before I actually have time to think about what I'm doing, or going to say, I walk up behind her.

"Whinny" She turns around.

"Michael, hi" I can sense Jasmine watching me from the other end of the table and I can also feel Avery watching me.

"Your eye's looking much better."

"Finally, it's taken a lot of ice."

"Well I still promise; I'll get even for you."

"Whatever you want to think. I mean if that helps you sleep at night." She says sarcastically.

"Oh, so you don't believe me?"

She laughs "I told you I can take care of myself."

I point to her eye "so what mark did you leave on the other person then?" This time she laughs, actually laughs out loud to where the other end of the table can hear her.

"Okay, point well made."

I raise my eyebrows at her and smile "I just wanted to say good luck tonight."

"Aren't you the one who needs the luck?"

"Possibly, but your cheering helps, and I know you do builds with Jimmy, which of course is risky behavior." This time I get to be the sarcastic one.

"Ha, ha well thank you."

"Yup." I start to walk away feeling like an idiot.

"Hey, Michael"

"Yeah." I say turning back around.

"Good luck to you. I promise I'll say a cheer just for you. And I promise to tell Jimmy to take it easy with the stunts that way, ya know, you won't have to hurt him or anything." She says playfully, then smiles again showing off her teeth.

"How thoughtful of you."

"Come here for a second." She pats the open space next to her. I think my heart skips a beat. Whinny telling me to come to her? I walk over and sit down.

"Is everything okay with your mom?"

"Oh, yeah I guess. She's been a little distant lately, but she's fine, I'm fine, you're fine. I guess everything is just fine."

"Fine is a very bland word." I look at her. Her eyes just mesmerize me. I have this feeling tonight's game is going to go well. Whinny will be there and knowing she'll be there comforts me.

I don't say anything to her comment. "Well then carry on good sir, I shan't distract you any more before the big game."

"I take it everything between us is fine?" When been playful with each other for the moment, but that doesn't necessarily mean the air is clear. I remember her being mad Tuesday, but I was the reason for it.

"I'd say it's better than fine." I smile at her, feeling myself want to take her in my arms and just disappear for a while. It seems like no one else even exists.

"Alright then." I get up and start walking for the doors out of the cafeteria. I don't know why it feels so hard to walk away from Whinny. Maybe it's because I never know when I'm going to see her next. I always feel like that might be the last time I get to talk to her. It's strange to feel this way considering I really don't know anything about her.

I feel like an idiot for just walking up to Whinny to say good luck for no apparent reason, but I needed that. I needed to know things between us are good since we haven't talked since Tuesday and I felt bad with the way things were left. I needed to hear her voice, it calms me. For some reason now I'm feeling more confident and I'm hoping this feeling stays with me going into tonight's game.

I hold the football in my hands, feeling the leather. I'm in my element, first game of the season and it couldn't have come soon enough. I finally feel at home. I finally feel okay, like everything that happened within this past year has just been forgotten, at least for this short time I'll be playing. I glance over at the cheerleaders and see Whinny up in the air, the crowd eager to follow along with the cheer. As the congregation chants our school name I step onto the field with a few of my other teammates and head to the center for the coin toss.

"Last first game we'll ever play together. Let's make it a hell of a good one!"

We won the coin toss and choose to receive. The game flies by, but is also boring. By the end of the first quarter we are up 21-0. And before going into halftime we're up 28-0. After halftime coach lets most of the J.V. kids play. I threw three touchdown passes, one to Shane, one to a junior and one to Parker. Lance ran in for one and basically the underdogs took it from there, although we didn't score any more touchdowns. It feels good to win so easily. But then again our season's always start like this, we play the easy teams first like our warm up games then mid-season it starts to get tougher.

Once in the locker room coach is eager to start his speech.

"Alright boys, good game. They should all be that easy. You all have worked very hard this summer and deserve to win. There was great leadership out on the field seniors. Now let's display that off the field. Underdogs you did great on defense, offense, we'll work on it. I hope you all are on your best behavior this weekend. Now let's get out of here."

We all shower and change as fast as we can. Everyone is excited to get to the next stage of the night, the party on top of the school roof even though we have to wait for all the parental fans to leave. When I head out to the field I notice mom never came to the game. Usually at this time she and dad would come down to the end zone to talk to me. But I don't see her anywhere. I watch as everyone files out of the bleachers and takes their conversations into the parking lot. For someone who has so much going for them, I've never felt so lost. My dad left us, mom won't talk to me, has barely said a word to me all week and won't tell me what's going on, obviously my right hand guy isn't here anymore and Jasmine and I aren't together. It's just not easy.

I hear some of the other guys come out and I watch as they head to their vehicles. All of them dressed in jeans and nice button down shirts. I guess it's that time so I pick up my bag and fall in behind them.

By the time I get there the roof is already hopping. I smile thinking it's crazy of us to do this. One of the guys on the team, his uncle is the janitor, and snagged the school keys one day and made a copy. Hence our great idea to have this party.

I have so much riding on this year and tonight could ruin everything for me, but at the same time a person's senior year only comes around one time. And I want to enjoy being a senior. Once I emerge from the stairwell I'm pushed and bumped by people everywhere. All the junior boys are following around Shane and Parker taking notes on how to do this for next year. We are officially legends. I start looking around and see Lance with his arm around Avery, for a split second I feel jealous.

"So what do you think?" Kevin comes up to me.

"I think it's a hell of a party and we're legends."

"Yeah I think so too."

"Where's Nancy?"

"I don't know."

"Something happen?"

"I asked her why she didn't come to the game. She told me she was with her cousin "Eric." He does the air quotes around Eric then pulls out his phone and goes into to his photos. He shows me a picture of Nancy kissing another guy.

"I'm guessing that's not her cousin."

"Me either, or else that's just gross."

"Why did she send you a picture of her makin' out with another guy?"

"She didn't. Some random number did."

"Well I guess she was tired of being ignored, she's going to take advantage of her new look and attitude."

"Yeah, who cares man? Its senior year, we're all heading in separate directions in a few months anyways. Why get tied down? I mean I'm glad I talked to her and got to know her since she's in my class, but I think I'm just going to have fun this year."

"Good for you." I really didn't want to think about all us guys going our separate ways, at least not yet.

"Come on let's go mingle." Kevin walks away, within an instant I'm surrounded by five girls.

"Good game Michael."

"You look so good in your uniform."

"Can I feel your muscles?" I feel like I can't breathe. The girls keep getting closer and closer.

"Girls, he's with me." I see Jasmine standing there in a short dress and her hair curled. The heard of girls depart all muttering things.

"Thanks."

"Well now that you and I aren't together every girl wants you. They want to seize this opportunity since, ya know they all thought we'd be together forever."

"Oh."

"I mean we are in the running for class cutest couple."

"I've heard." She smiles and we walk past throngs of people towards the punch bowl.

"You didn't wish me any luck cheering." I'm surprise she seems so calm, but she does cross her arms.

"You don't need it, you're the captain."

"You and Whinny?"

"Please." I laugh. "It's senior year. We're all going to be leaving in a few months. Why get tied down?" Yeah, I just stole Kevin's speech.

"Some people like it." She looks at me. I finally couldn't take looking her in the eyes any longer and turn away. When I don't say anything she speaks up. "Where are you going?"

"Don't know yet, you?"

"I don't know. I always told myself I was going to go where you choose."

"What? Why?"

"Because I loved you and I wanted to be with you, still do. The thought of college with you by my side never scared me, now it does." This is the Jasmine I had fallen for back freshman year, sweet, caring, willing to put others first but yet chase her own dreams. However, people change.

"I'm sorry."

"Me too. I really am changing Michael. I don't think you should completely close the door on us just yet." Shane comes dancing over and grabs my arm.

"It's our song. Sorry Jas, have to steal him." He drags me to where everyone is dancing. "Plus you kind of looked like you needed to be saved." I laugh as the other football guys come over and we all dance and sing along to the LOVE SHAK. I'm sure we look stupid but we're having a good time and we just won the first game of the season so it really doesn't matter.

After the song ends I decide to head home. I'm pulling an all day at work tomorrow and I really don't want to talk to Jasmine again. I feel bad about us ending, and I feel bad that she still has feelings, but I can't go back down that road. I also don't want to risk partying on the roof too long. It's awesome to say I'm part of it, just don't want to take advantage of it. I finally make my way through all the dancing crowds and to the door that leads downstairs. I notice Avery leaning against it alone.

"Tonight mid night."

"No thanks." I barely even look at her. I have a feeling Lance is standing close too, probably just setting me up. She grabs my arm.

"Michael." Her eyes are worried. I pull my arm back and open the door and leave. I had so much respect for Avery over the summer. Now I feel angry at her, just like the old days.

At home I climb up in the tree house my brother, father and I made. I look over at Whinny's house, it's dark. I lay back and look at the stars. Thinking about college scares me. We have no idea when my dad will come home and the thought of leaving my mom alone crushes me. But the University of Tennessee is looking promising, plus it's a big school which means if I would get a scholarship it'd be worth more.8 But so will tuition. Unfortunately, it takes a little over seven hours to get to Knoxville from here. I don't think I could leave mom alone with that much distance between us. It's not like I'm a baby that's still attached to my mom. I just know that with losing Max and dad not being around, this year hasn't been easy and if I move away she'll have no one.

"Michael?" I sit up and look over the side of the tree house. Whinny is standing underneath the tree.

"You scared the crap out of me."

She laughs easily. "Sorry."

"How'd you know I was up here?"

"I saw a figure climb in the tree from down the road and I was taking a wild guess that it wasn't your mom, but then again, I've been wrong before."

"Oh."

"Can I come up?" I'm surprised she even asks. Actually I'm a little surprised she's the one who made an effort to come talk to me. Does this mean she's warming up to me and she might actually believe our friendship is growing the same way I do?

"Well it's a no girl's allowed policy."

"Well I guess in that case goodnight."

"But that doesn't mean I can't come down." I say quickly, worried she might actually already be headed to her house. I start down the ladder. She's dressed in a black polo and nice khaki pants. Her hair is in a long braid descending down her back with kinky strands sticking out here and there.

"Well hopefully someday when you meet the right girl you'll take her up there, then you can come find me and take me up there." We both sit down and lean against the tree.

"You mean you actually want to see inside this old thing?"

"Who wouldn't? I watched you and your family build it. I was so jealous. You and Max would spend hours up there; I've been dying to know what's so great about it ever sense."

"Ha, we were young boys that's what was so great about it. And I could name a few."

"You mean Jasmine."

"Yeah" We both just sit here. "Sometimes I forget how much time I actually did spend with her."

"Time is such a valuable thing." There's silence, not awkward silence, just peaceful.

"Whinny, have you ever been in a relationship?" I'm surprised I asked it, but I won't lie, I'm beyond curious. I've never kept tabs on her or anything, I mean I'll be honest I pretty much forgot about her.

"Do you know Ian, from the wrestling team?"

"Yeah."

"Well, we dated for seven months and then he cheated on me. That was sophomore year, ever since I haven't really put a lot of trust into anybody besides myself."

"Not all guys are like that though."

"I realize that, but I also haven't really met anyone that's just blown me away. I've been working and cheering and I'm content with that. I don't need a guy in my life to make me happy. And I'm not the type of person to just give my heart to anyone. I'm not too worried, this is a small town, but it's not the only town or city for that matter."

How could she be worried, she's pretty much every guy's dream girl, an athletic girl with an amazing personality, and good looks?

"I'm surprised though he doesn't seem like that type of guy." I'm a little shocked over that. Ian's the quietest guy I've ever known, well until you get him on the wrestling mat. But looking at him you'd think he was harmless.

She gives me a look.

"What?"

She shakes her head "nothing."

"No, tell me." She doesn't say anything. I want to ask again.

"Not everybody comes off as great, or bad as they seem. What you see on the outside isn't always what you'll get on the inside. Remember, looks can be deceiving and you should never judge something or someone based on the outside." I listen to what she said and think about it.

"Also, temptation can be a devastating thing." Temptation… I wonder why she gave me that look? She obviously knows something I don't.

"If you don't mind me asking, how did you find out?"

She snorts. "I walked in on him and this girl, in the girl's locker room."

"Ok, that's gross."

"You know surprisingly they aren't the only two I've caught in there."

"Whinny." I say playfully "Too much info now."

"You ask I'll tell." She smiles. "A lot of people like to do it, ya know after school practices when they think they're the last to leave."

"Ooohh" I fall over into the grass. "You're killing me, stop. I don't need a mental image." I'm laughing as I sit back up.

Whinny laughs too "I don't want to have to go through all this alone." I look at her and actually understand what she means. It's nice for her to share this information with me, even though it's information I could go without.

"Good game tonight." She says changing the subject.

"Thank you and I must say your cheering was ravishing." She chuckles and looks at me. Her eye is looking better than at lunch but even in the dark I can still see the black underneath it. There's something about her eyes, I can never look away. I should learn from this moment to never look her in the eyes again, but at the same time it feels like a safe place. It feels like where I want to be. We stare at each other for a moment. I can tell she's trying to read me, I always feel so open and vulnerable when she looks at me like this.

"So how was the party on the roof?" She asks making the moment light again.

"I must say it was pretty epic."

"Dang, I was hoping it would have been like the Titanic."

"What?" I find myself smiling for no apparent reason then I realize I've been smiling throughout our entire conversation.

"A sinking ship." She informs me.

"Oh, ha. Well I would hope it wouldn't have been that dramatic."

"Only for a few."

"Oh I'm sure some stuff probably went down, and no I'm not talking about undergarments." We both crack up.

When I finally catch my breath I ask "were you working I presume?"

"Yes, waitressing down at the Frying Pan."

"Fun"

"It pays. The tips are great. Everybody knows me since it's a small town." She leans her shoulder into me, I feel a slight zing. "So if the party was so epic, why aren't you still there?" I can tell she's giving me a look as if to say 'the party mustn't have been that great'.

"I didn't want to be. I didn't want to risk getting caught."

"Yeah, no offense but it was kind of a stupid idea."

I laugh "I know; we just want to be awesome senior leaders."

"You do realize there are better, smarter ways to being awesome senior leaders?"

"Well... yeah, but."

"Like winning sectionals perhaps, and maybe being nice to people in the hallways at school that aren't popular, or even volunteering at a charity event. Show the younger kids that it's okay to be nice and to help others. To me that's what a great leader does."

What she just said kind of shocks me, in a good way. "I'm not mean to people in the hallways."

"Maybe not, but do you go out of your way to be nice to them?"

"Well I have friends in almost every click of every grade."

"Because you're popular, and mainly because our school loves football and you happen to be one of the most important members of our team."

"Ouch." I put my hand over my heart "that hurt."

"But I think you have great potential to leave this school with the people remembering you by the outstanding things you did not only on the field, but also off." She lightly touches my elbow and holds on. I get the chills. I'm thinking about what she just said, I realize she gave me a compliment.

I turn my head and look at her "thanks Whinny." We sit starring at each other for a long moment. I can feel the electric running through us. Both of us start to lean in for a kiss, when she turns her head quickly. I lean my head down. Were we really about to kiss and if so why did she suddenly pull away?

There's a moment of silence before she says "you have something heavy on your mind don't you?" She asks looking onward again. I still have my head down.

"How do you know?" I finally pull back myself.

"Most people like to be alone when they really want to think and sometimes they'll revisit a special place that brings back memories." She's good.

"You always read me don't you?" She finally let's go of my arm, although I wish she wouldn't have.

"I read everyone Michael; it's just something I do. I don't mean it in a bad way, I just pick up on people's posture and body language."

"I'm just thinking about college"

"And?"

"I don't know what I want to do."

"What feels most right for you?"

"I don't know." I lean my head back against the tree, I really just don't know. "Playing football, I mean I don't know what I want to study as my major."

"You will, in time. It's still the first month of school, heck it's technically still the first week, you've got time to figure it out. Maybe one day in class you'll feel inspired by something you learn and that'll be it."

"You're always so optimistic." I give her a nudge with my shoulder and laugh. "What about you?" I look at her; she's looking onward again.

"Something along the lines of writing and journalism, although I'd really like to be an author someday."

"Very nice, how did you decide on that?"

"I just like to write, it's when I feel most free and the happiest."

"That sounds like me and football. Have you decided where you're going?" Right as I ask mom pulls up. She sure is out late for a Friday night.

"Hello Michael, Whinny." Mom stutters slightly when she says Whinny's name. She looks pale again, and seems ancy. Whinny stands up and I follow her lead, sad that I'm guessing this means our conversation is over.

"Nice to see you again Mrs. Statemen." Mom just nods and quickly turns towards the house.

"I better be off, night Michael" Whinny starts walking towards her own house.

"Night Whinny" Mom already has our door unlocked and is inside.

I follow her "what was that about?" I ask as I close the door behind me.

"What was what?"

"You look like you've just seen a ghost when talking to Whinny. Just Monday you were rooting for me to be with her."

"It was nothing Michael I have no idea what you're talking about." She walks towards the kitchen and back towards her room. She's been distant and off since Tuesday.

"Hey mom?"

"What?" Her voice tight.

"I don't know what's going on with you and I don't know if you're okay, you won't talk to me. But I want you to know that I'm here and I need you. You're my mom. So please don't give up and keep me out in the cold, we'll get through whatever this is together." She looks at me with tears in her eyes; I walk away towards the stairs so I can go to bed myself. I have too much girl crap going on in my life. It's at moments like this when I wish Max was here, or dad.

Chapter Five

The next morning I'm at work by seven. And by noon I have sweated my butt off in this August heat. I have push mowed three large yards, trimmed landscaping at two places and painted shutters for Mr. and Mrs. Hinder, plus took Mrs. Rains dog for a walk and that's not part of my job. She's just such a sweet old lady with no family around. I finally sit down on the ground, leaning against my truck tire and start to eat my sandwich when my cell rings. It's from an unfamiliar number which can only mean one thing.

"Dad!"

"Hey son."

"Man it's good to hear from you."

"I know it's been too long."

"So how are things overseas?"

"Busy."

"I know you can't say too much."

He laughs, "what about football?"

"We had our first game last night. We blew the other team out of the water."

"That's my boy, any touchdowns for you?"

"I threw three."

"Great job!"

"Thanks, we've been practicing a lot to be ready for this season."

"Sergeant let's go." I hear someone call in the background.

"I got to go Michael, Have a great season! Love you."

"Love you too dad." There was a click before I finished. I sigh. It's been three weeks since I've talked to dad and that was the best conversation we'll probably have for another three weeks. Occasionally he'll write but mostly it's to mom.

I honestly have no idea what to do about mom. The other night she freaked out over what, I have no idea and last night she couldn't stand being around Whinny and was out till almost midnight. I wonder if this has anything to do with Whinny's black eye? I finish eating and get back up. Maybe if I'm lucky I'll get all the stops done at a decent hour today.

Getting done at a decent hour didn't work. I'm pulling in my driveway at eight. A thirteen-hour day is nice but having to do everything manually sucks. If we had a riding mower it wouldn't be so bad, or maybe if we didn't actually have to trim people's landscaping or fix their gutters and paint their shutters. But it's good money and normally I work throughout the week so I don't have to do it all at once like today. I've had this job since I was fourteen and even though I complain about it I know I'll miss it. I get out of my dodge pick-up and grab my lunch box off the back.

"Michael." Avery's voice rings out, scaring me.

"Avery you scared the crap out of me." I turn; before I have time to react she throws her arms around me and embraces me in a hug.

"Tell me you want to be with me." She cries. For some reason I look over at Whinny's house. There are a few lights on for once. Avery pulls back and I look at her.

"How did Lance know that I came over to your house?"

"What?"

"Don't play dumb please."

"I didn't tell him that much, I swear."

"Why would you even tell him anything?"

"So he would back off. I mean he asked me out Michael. Don't you get it, I like you, and I want to be with you!"

"Avery, you told me you like him too."

"I do Michael, a little. But we have so much more time and feelings invested in this already. I'd like to see it through; I'd like to know if it would work between us as a real couple."

"Hey guys." We both turn and see Whinny walking up the street, dressed in her waitressing attire.

"Whinny." I say. Avery just stands here placing her hands on her hips.

This moment could not get any more awkward, which I don't even know why it is in the first place. Maybe because I came close to kissing Whinny last night? But Avery doesn't know that.

"Alright well I can see I interrupted something so I'm going to go. Goodnight." Whinny starts walking the rest of the way to her house.

"Didn't feel like being polite?"

"Oh please Michael, you know I'm not overly kind to anyone."

"No, I think it's more just the girls in our class. You seem to be getting along just fine with the guys." Avery gives me a look.

"Ask me out, I don't know what you are so afraid of."

"Lance is my friend and I won't do this to him."

"I told him it had nothing to do with you, it was all me. I told him we saw each other over the summer and that I still had feelings for you and wanted to see where it would go. And we don't have to announce to the world that we're dating yet, I just want to be with you Michael, without having to hide it." She leans up and we kiss. The thoughts of summer come flooding back to me, escaping everything else from my mind. This is my chance to see, I mean why not try things with Avery, if it doesn't work out it doesn't, but I don't want to spend my time thinking what if. She's right we should see this through, on some occasions opposites do attract.

"Avery." I smile at her after we finish our kiss, "will you be my girlfriend?"

"Yes! Geeze what took you so long?" I give her a playful look then pick her up and carry her to the front porch. "Then let's go inside, let me shower, we'll eat and watch a movie."

"I really like the sound of that."

The rest of the night is perfect. Mom is home for once so the three of us ate together and mom entertained Avery while I took my shower and by ten Avery and I were on the couch watching BRUCE ALMIGHTY because that's her favorite movie. For the beginning of the movie we sat next to each other holding hands, half way through I put my arm around her and she laid her head on my shoulder, and by the end she still had her head on my shoulder but also had her feet over my lap. It felt nice getting to be with her and touch and hold her. But nice? I'm not sure that's what it should feel like when you're with the one you really want to be with. I know we agreed to try things but I still feel like something's holding me back.

After the movie I take her home. We ride in silence for the short three-minute trip.

"I know we're together now, but let's keep it low for a while, I know this has got to be hard on Lance."

She smiles "that's fine with me." I give her a kiss and head back home. I really feel like I've stabbed Lance in the back but at the same time Avery and I were kind of together first. I'm tired of over thinking and trying to please other people.

All day Sunday I spend to myself. Well sort of, mom asked for me to take care of the chores around the house while she ran errands, another day of not getting to see her. I know I shouldn't complain since she was home last night, but one night out of seven really doesn't cut it.

Avery called and asked if I wanted to come over but it was my one free day, plus I had homework so I opted out. Maybe that was wrong of me, shouldn't I want to be with her every possible second? I think I'm still use to the summer and how we kept things low key.

But either way my Sunday was perfect. I went outside a couple times after mowing the yard hoping to catch Whinny, just to talk and to apologize for last night, but that was a no go. It's like Whinny moves with the wind, she comes and goes and if you aren't paying attention you'll miss her. The thought of the next time I'll see Whinny again puts a smile on my face. Here she had been next door this whole time and I was too much of a jackass to notice. But now things are different. Now we know each other exist and within just three times of talking—which weren't even that long—we built a friendship.

I made some hamburgers on the grill and set the table, mom was speechless when she got home. She's not use to anyone using the grill other than dad.

"Wow Michael, you made us dinner, thank you." She says as we sit down to eat.

"It's the least I could do, you've been busy all day and I was home, so I figured why not."

"You are going to be just fine on your own at school."

"I know." I stir around my cottage cheese with my fork. She seems a little better, but this past week with her has been a bear. "Did I tell you dad called yesterday?"

"He did? No you didn't mention it."

"I guess in the excitement of Avery and me, I forgot."

"What did he say?" She asks cautiously.

"Not much actually, it wasn't even a two-minute conversation."

"Well honey it's the thought that counts."

"I know." I look at mom. "How are you?"

She finally looks up "I'm fine honey, really. You don't have to worry about me. Instead you need to worry about your grades and homework." She launches into a typical mother speech and I drown her out. I guess I'll take her word for it.

"and the last thing I'll say, is that I think Avery is okay." That part got my attention.

"Okay?"

"I mean I can definitely see how you two are opposites. Opposites can sometimes attract, so I guess you'll just have to see how it goes. Just remember to follow what your heart tells you. It does more talking than you realize. It's whether or not you have the courage to listen to it."

Wow, that's probably the first and most powerful thing mom's said to me in months. "I guess. You realize that's the girl I hung out with most of the summer?"

"I did not, but it sounds like you've already got a foundation started that's always a plus."

She gets up and starts cleaning up the dinner mess. I'm glad mom is okay with me and Avery, that's better than me and Jasmine.

Avery and I keep things cool the next day; it's as if nothing ever happened. During homeroom she sits on her side and I sit in the middle. Jasmine thankfully doesn't try talking to me, hopefully she's finally getting the idea that she and I will not be getting back together even though it's only the second week of school. She glances at me a lot but I keep my head down and act as if I don't notice.

I go to all my classes, although I'll admit it feels weird to be with someone but to not be with someone. I don't think I've ever been with a girl where we were considered together but couldn't be seen with each other, at least not yet. But then again the only other girl I've really been with has been Jasmine. At lunch I sit next to Lance.

"Hey dude, are you okay?"

"I'm fine."

"I really didn't mean too."

"Please don't get all sentimental with me."

"Okay. But I know the feelings you have for her are real and I feel like a huge jackass."

"Look Michael, yeah it sucks but I'll get over it, there are other girls in this school. Avery told me you two had been seeing each other over the summer so whatever, you had dibs first anyways. As long as she's happy. I'm just surprised you couldn't man up and tell me yourself."

"Because I thought she and I ended things that's why I didn't. But then last week we kept meeting up and we just finally decided we need to see this through. I just don't want you to hold anything against me. We've been bros since first grade."

"Nah man, if we've been bro's that long than you should know me better than that. You would know that I'm not like that, even if you do get any girl you want." Lance starts talking with Kevin sitting across from him and I get the message that this conversation is through. I was hoping after talking to Lance that I'd feel some relief; I think the feeling is actually worse.

We hit the drills hard today at practice. Coach said he wants us to perfect the little things that most teams overlook, like handoffs, short passes, blocks, and being ready for a blitz. "Before you can play with the big boys you got to know the technique" is coaches' famous saying. It was a long, hot, and tedious work out, but we finally made it to the scrimmage. I'm sitting out waiting to go back in, and find myself watching the cheerleaders or I guess more specifically Whinny. She's partner stunting with Jimmy. I'm amazed at how she can do a back flip into his hands and he'd raise her into a lift, it looks painful.

Right now he's holding her one handed, she's got one-foot-high in the air, he moves and she puts her other foot down so now two handed. He throws her in the air, she does a 360 back flip and boom, falls hard onto the track. I instantly jump off the bench unaware of what I'm doing. Kevin grabs my jersey.

"Dude."

"What?" But even as I ask this I know what he's thinking. Jimmy's attempting to help Whinny back up, she sits there a second, just looking at him and shaking her head.

"Get up Whinny" I say under my breath, but I'm pretty sure Kevin overheard me. Jimmy kneels down next to her, puts his arm around her and pulls her up. She stands hunched over and they talk for a minute. She straightens, turns around; within two seconds he hoists her high in the air again.

"Alright offense, get in there and show them how it's done." Coach grabs my helmet. "Remember the handoffs we just worked on."

"Yes sir."

"Good." He let's go and I run out to the field. We work right down the field with ease.

"That's it, practice over. DEFENSE!" coach yells. This means practice is over for everyone but the defense.

I'm sitting on the bench in the locker room after changing my clothes. Kevin walks in, he likes being the last one to leave the field, and it's been his thing since freshmen year. Every practice and every game he likes to just take a moment I guess.

"Man my practice clothes reek. I've got to wash them tonight." I say putting them inside my bag.

"No doubt, I usually have mom do it though."

"Mom's never home, I'm really starting to get worried. She's been working a lot but she's also been acting weird. I can't describe it. I honestly feel like I have no parents right now."

"She's probably going through the change, no biggie man." I laugh, I guess it could be that, but I think it has more to do with our family situation. I just don't know how much or what of it yet. "So you have to tell me, you and Avery? For real?"

"What's wrong with it? Lance told you didn't he? I bet he's pissed off at me."

"I think he's more upset with the fact that you didn't man up and tell him, but yes he told me, and gross. You two use to despise each other."

"People change, and it's not like she's ugly or anything."

"Yeah okay, it's just like you went from miss prissy pants to miss gothic dark ages. It's weird. And then what's the deal with Whinny?" I stare at him, my heart's racing all of a sudden.

"What about Whinny?"

"I don't know, that's why I'm asking. I mean yeah Jimmy dropped her; she's probably use to it, but man you sure did fly off that bench. You looked like you wanted to kick his ass."

"There's nothing to tell." I shrug my shoulders.

"Come on man, I know you way better than that, I get it you're into two chicks, hell maybe even more. I mean you were with Jasmine for a long time. Now you're just playing the field"

"Ha, I don't know about that. Avery and I hung out all summer, there was no one else."

"No one else, until now."

I look at him, maybe's he's right.

"So you really hung out with Avery all summer?"

"Yeah, none of you knew and neither did our parents." We didn't do anything, I'd just

sneak over to her house and we'd sit outside talking. I guess I'm hoping that with us being "official" that maybe we'll start going out and doing things. I miss her, and I get jealous when I see Lance with her. But I don't know, I don't have that "I want to be with her 24/7 feeling like when I was with Jas."

"I think you know what the real answer is. I mean it's good to date people and find out what you like but let's face it if you don't feel those vibes then it's never going to work. Besides you just came off a long relationship anyways, why try and force something?"

I look over at him, for someone who's never been in a long term relationship Kevin gives pretty good advice. "But what if it could be something great, and I miss out on it because I didn't give it a chance?"

"You guys always give me crap because I'm never with someone for a long period of time, that's because it starts out fun but then the longer we're together I just realize I don't have as strong of feelings as I thought. So we break up and I move on. Honestly you and Avery have been together for a while, all summer. And those vibes aren't there, yet they never will be. Nothing will change just because now you're official."

"I never thought of it like that, I just thought you got bored and wanted a new chase."

"I'm a better person than that, come on Michael." He slaps my back. "I'm not saying that things with Avery won't go well or that you shouldn't give it a chance. I'm just saying if you feel like you're forcing everything now, you'll always feel that way. Remember those intense feelings you had for Jas, I think you have those for Whinny. Just a brief observation." Kevin heads off for the showers and leaves me to ponder on what he's said.

I grab my duffel bag and walk out of the locker room. As I come back out to the field I notice Whinny sitting on the bleachers. I realize I want to see her and spend time with her, so I head over.

"Hey."

"Hey Michael" She rubs her neck, track scratches run down the side of her face and left arm. She looks exhausted. I sit down next to her.

"Whinny what's your favorite color?"

"Turquoise."

"Want to know mine?"

She doesn't say anything just looks at me. I can tell she's not feeling this conversation, but I tell her anyways. "Blue."

"Royal, Caribbean, Aqua…? These are very important things to know." That broke her mood, she's optimistic again.

"That's a tough one, but I'd say Royal."

"I'll be sure to wrap birthday gift in that color then." She rubs her neck some more. Then sits there, looking lifeless.

"You need a ride home?"

"Nope" She slowly starts pulling off her shoes and socks throwing them into her bag.

"Oh. Okay then." I stand and hoist my bag over my shoulder. I turn to walk away.

"But I could use a ride to work." I look back at her and she smiles at me.

"Do you ever take a break?"

"Hardly ever, I told you it's always go go go." She slips on some flip flops. I hold out my hand to help her up and she takes it. It's tiny and sweaty and her nails are painted purple. Even though it's a brief interaction, it's intense.

"Well let's go then." We start across the field. "Are you okay?" She's walking stiff and with a slight limp.

"What do you mean?"

"I saw Jimmy drop you, you fell from a high height, but I guess you're use to that. You know you did fall from a tree."

She laughs "It happens, I'm fine, thanks."

"Okay well then completely switching topics, I'm sorry for the other night when Avery gave you the evil eye." She stops walking and laughs. "What? I'm being serious?" But I'm laughing too. I realize what I just said sounds lame. I feel like everything I say to Whinny is lame. She probably wonders how I got the status quo I do have.

"Well thank you, but I get it. I understand why I was given the 'evil eye'" and we're back moving.

"Why?"

"Come on Michael, you're the best looking guy in school by far, the most athletic and believe it or not, you're one of the sweetest and now your single. She's making her move and she doesn't want anyone else too, it's a jealousy thing. All girls go through it. Jasmine was really bad with you; you were just too nice to realize it."

"Sweetest, I thought the other day you told me I was mean to people."

She rolls her eyes slightly "come on Michael, I never said you were mean, I just meant that you're a great leader and if anyone can turn this school around and get different clicks to hang out with each other, it could be you."

"Thanks, Whinny, but really I'm not that great."

She gives me a sweet smile. "You may not think so but every other girl does."

"Well thank you." I want to ask her what her opinion of me is.

"Oh and congrats I guess it turns out you really aren't single anymore" We get to my truck and I throw my bag on back.

"Wait, how do you know that?" Avery and I agreed we weren't going to really tell anyone or announce to world that we're together yet. I mean yeah a few guys on the football team know and I'm sure her close friends do, but Whinny? How would she know?

"Her Facebook status."

"What?" I haven't been on Facebook in forever, this thought scares me.

We climb in and we both just sit there a second. "Yeah it was "happiest girl in the world, summer romance picking up right where we left off, finally got my man, wonderful Michael Statemen" My jaw drops. I can't believe she posted that on Facebook, poor Lance. So much for keeping things down low, now everyone knows. I start up the truck, roll down the windows and we're off.

"Guess the cat's out of the bag then. I thought it was only my friends who knew"

"Oh turn here."

"This isn't the way to the Frying Pan."

"I'm working at the Humane Society today."

"Do you ever miss home?"

"No. I like it that way." She turns her head and leans it back against the seat. When I look at her all I see are the track burns running down her face. Surprisingly her complexion still looks pure and genuine. She slides her feet out of the flip flops, pulls them up and puts them on my dash. For some reason I don't mind.

My mind flashes to Avery during the summer; we never went anywhere actually so I'd never seen this side of her, just relaxed. Avery was always hyped up about something, like a book she just read or something she heard on the news or some type of new drama that was happening within her family.

Within an instant my eyes are back on Whinny, she has her eyes closed. I smile and turn the radio on, lean back in my seat and just drive. Ten minutes later I pull into the parking lot to the Humane Society. Whinny's sitting up pulling her hair out of a bun and putting it back into another one.

"Do you need a ride home tonight?"

"No, but thanks for the ride here" She opens the door, gets out and takes a few steps.

"It'll be dark, and that's a long walk." She looks at her phone and instantly something changes. She doesn't move for what seems like an eternity.

"Whinny, are you alright?" Finally, she turns back toward the truck dropping her bag. She stands there and it's like we're having a starring contest. She walks back up to the window.

"Why are you so worried about me?"

I smile. "I wish I knew."

"Well stop Michael." Her facial expression is cold and serious all of a sudden.

"I don't think it's that easy."

"It's going to have to be. You now have a girlfriend and two weeks ago you could have cared less about me. So I'm sure it won't be too hard to find who you were two weeks ago and be that person again." She snaps.

My smile fades. "Whinny."

"I think we shouldn't talk to each other for a while." She turns and starts back to the entrance doors. I jump out of the truck and head around the front.

"Whinny wait" She looks back at me one last time and wipes away a tear before going inside. I lean against my passenger side door. What on earth just happened?

Chapter Six

The rest of the week goes by slowly. Whinny keeps her distance, I haven't seen her all week, or if I did, she was gone before I could approach. I went over once but her mom said she was working. I really can't figure out why I care so much. I spent ten years ignoring her and acting as if she never existed and now after spending one week with her, I feel like it's the end of the world that she's mad at me and doesn't want me around anymore. I don't understand what's going on.

I had gone over to Avery's Tuesday and Wednesday after I got off work. We talked like usual about anything and everything besides sports. It was hard because in all honesty the only thing I've been thinking about is the game Friday. It's only our second game and we are already playing a team in our conference, we never play a conference team this early.

But it means so much to Avery to steer clear of those topics so I did. She talked about school and the classes she was taking— none of which I am—and she talked about her friends and her parent's. She talked about the latest book she's reading, and if she wanted to start a garden next spring what she wanted to plant. I knew I wasn't much of a conversationalist; I was tired from football and work, so I just tried to be an empathetic listener. I found myself actually fairly bored with our conversations. What was it about these that had caught my eye this summer? Then I wondered if it was the other way around. Maybe I met Avery and she was the one who took my loneliness away and it was Whinny who I had the real feelings for.

I still can't believe Avery had lead Lance on and so quickly just dropped him. That Facebook status had probably really hurt him, although he never said anything about it and that's in the past, so now I just move forward.

At school Avery and I are slowly coming around. I sit next to her in homeroom, Jasmine just glares, and then I walk her to her classes, but by lunch we separate. I always sit with the guys and Avery sits with her friends and we don't really see each other the rest of the day. We haven't started any PDA and I seem to be more than okay with that. Some of the guys are still giving me a hard time about ending up with her anyways.

But now it's finally Friday and lunch time, which is always the best. It's the only time us guys are all together at once.

"So I'm thinking we start tonight's game off slow, make it suspenseful then go in for the kill. Plus, we'll get to play more." Parker says.

"Yeah but what if we wait too long and can't pull off the win?" Joe questions.

"You doubt us?" Everyone starts throwing around comments.

Kevin finally speaks. "I say we play. We go out and stomp everyone right away. It's conference! Besides we want to show everyone that we are a team they don't want to mess around with."

"Agreed, we aren't going to be stupid and risk this." I look at each one of them. I love the guys but hopefully they won't be this stupid tonight. "We have worked way too hard to just dick around. We go out and win within the first half." I glance over to the cheerleaders table. Whinny's sitting there. I want to go over to her, she looks defeated for some reason. I want to see her smile and see the optimistic/ positive side of her, but I realize I have a girlfriend now. I look over to Avery who's reading a book. She's the one I should go over to.

After school I wait for Avery by her locker. She's taking her sweet time which is pushing me for mine.

"Wow, I think this is the first."

"Don't get used to it. You know every day I'm usually at practice, but today I'm going home to eat and get my stuff for tonight's game." I close her locker door for her after she's finished. As we walk out to the parking lot she takes my hand. I don't take my hand away but as of now it still feels too weird in this environment.

"Good luck tonight."

"Thanks, are you coming?"

She gives me a look. "Michael I hate sports, you know that, so why would you even ask?"

"Yeah but just one, and it's for me, to support me."

"Maybe later this year, but no promises" I lean in and give her a kiss on the check.

"Be careful on your way home." I start towards my truck. I like Avery I really do. I'm just use to knowing that someone who supports me is always at a game. Whether it's my dad, mom, brother, all three or just Jasmine, but tonight none of that is happening. I already know mom can't make it, dads of course not around and Jasmine and I aren't together.

"Hey Michael" I open my truck door as Whinny approaches all decked out in her cheerleading uniform. A smile spreads across my face, this is the first time I've seen or talked to her since Monday.

"Miss Peterson, what can I do for you?"

She gives me a small smile. "You can play well tonight." She seems to be in a better mood than at lunch.

"Thanks, I'll sure try, but what if I don't?" It honestly feels good to hear her voice and to see her. I take a few steps closer to her.

"Well I don't know. I guess kiss any other good lucks from me goodbye. I'd feel like you're a jinx or something." Now she smirks and I can tell she's back.

"I don't want that, so expect a hell of a game." I step closer to her, she smiles.

"Will do."

"Do you need a ride?" I ask as Jimmy comes pulling up in his mustang.

"I'm good, but thanks." She gets in and the two drive off. She really is pushing this 'us keeping our distance thing' but at least she made an attempt to come talk to me. That is definitely a pick me up after Avery saying she won't come to a game just because she hates sports.

At home mom's not there, she left a note saying good luck, play hard and have fun. I wad it up and throw it away. I'm over mom not being a mom. I can't even begin to imagine what she's doing out all the time. After this past weekend she's pretty much been gone and distant all week again. I head upstairs and pack my stuff. I glance through my window and happen to see Whinny heading out her front door. I want so desperately to catch up with her, just to spend some time with her, but technically I have a girlfriend.

Chapter Seven

I was given my sign. And now I realize that I'm an idiot and should have realized this a week ago, but hey I'm a guy and sometimes we just make really stupid mistakes. But my mom's right if you listen to your heart, it'll tell you what you want. Again I'm sure it was telling me long before this what I wanted, I just didn't have to courage to listen, until now.

Maybe I should back up just a bit here. We're in the second quarter moving down field towards the end zone. Both of us teams are scoreless.

"Let's run an option route to Lance, down the right sideline."

"You want to go right? We always go left with that play."

"Exactly so let's throw them off. Break!"

"99 South, 77 orange, North Carolina, HIKE!" I fake hand off to Quincy, and give the ball to Lance. He breaks free and is heading down the right sidelines. Two guys from the other team's defense comes out of nowhere, both built like freight trains. "Run Lance!" I yell following him up the sideline. I'm back about fifteen feet, but it's too late. Both guys push and jump towards him. They all go flying out of bounds and into the cheerleaders. Our cheerleaders. What's worse is Jimmy just threw Whinny in the air and he gets tackled. And everything else just happens in slow motion it seems. Whinny finishes doing her splits and is on the way down with no one to catch her. Half the cheerleading team has been taken out and the other half standing are freaking out, because football guys are in their domain. Jimmy's trying to get up, but is caught under one of the other players. I start running towards her but realize it's too late. She's already hit the ground, her body already thrown off, she lands mostly on her back. I stop and quickly help Lance to his feet, he's a bit shaken up too.

"You alright?"

"Yeah." Then I reach Whinny, I'm the first one here.

Silent tears are streaming down her face. I rip my helmet off.

"You're going to be okay, it's okay Whinny, just breathe, take deep breaths and breathe." She doesn't listen; she's wincing in pain, holding her breath and now barely making a sound. Her face is starting to turn red.

"Whinny." I take her hand. "You just got the air knocked out of you, it's okay but you have to calm down."

"Get a paramedic someone please." And the cheerleading coach is next to me. Jimmy's kneeling next to her now too. The crowd is beyond silent. Lance stands next to me.

"Everyone back up, give her some air please."

"Michael come on, we have a game we have to play." Our coach comes over and puts a hand on my shoulder. "She'll be okay; the paramedics are on their way."

"Yeah, I'm coming." Before I get up I lean down and whisper in Whinny's ear. "I'm always going to be here for you, no matter how hard to try to push me away. Now take deep breaths please Whinny, you have too and I'll see you soon." I start to walk away with Lance, then look back one last time, even though she's in an immense amount of pain it's like she heard me, because even with tears in her eyes I can tell she's looking at me. I put my helmet back on and head back to the guys. I feel even more desire to kick this team's ass now.

"Lance you alright?" Kevin asks.

"I'm good. I want to run that play again, only with a lateral, Michael follow me."

"Break!"

"Blue 42 hut hut!" This time the plays works perfectly. The same defenders come out of nowhere, but this time we were expecting it, Lance waits until the defense gets close then tosses the ball back to me, I'm about ten yards behind him. I jump over the guys as they crash to the ground thinking they stopped the play. Open field the rest of the way and I complete the last fifteen yards for a touchdown.

"You were right." I smack his helmet.

"Hell yeah! Let's go!"

Half time came rolling around and we all headed to the locker room. I looked over and noticed Whinny was gone. Coach came in and gave us an update, then started talking about the game plan for the second half. I tuned out, I was concentrating on Whinny. Apparently, they took her to the hospital to make sure nothing was broke, but they were expecting her to be back cheering by the fourth quarter.

And that was my sign, my heart basically stopped beating when I saw Whinny falling from the air, and it crushed me to walk away from her when I knew she was in so much pain. It was a sign that I knew I liked her and cared for her more than any other girl I've ever met. Suddenly I felt lighter.

And to now, we won 14-7, it was great competition, and we older guys got to play the whole game. I threw one touchdown pass to Kevin and ran in for the second. Joe was pretty pumped he got a sack on the quarterback tonight. I'd say we played but we didn't play really well. I finish stuffing everything inside my bag; this is the first time I'm the last to leave the locker room. Kevin usually is, but I'm guessing he's still out on the field reminiscing about the game.

And of course everyone else wants to hurry and get gone because we seniors and seniors only are having a party out at Jacob's cabin. I'm not sure if I want to go or not. Avery sent me a text saying 'come over after the game.' I'm tired of just going over to her house and talking. I'm a pretty outgoing type of guy so this is getting old, fast. Besides I know that Avery and I can't see each other anymore. I know with how I reacted to what happened to Whinny wasn't a normal reaction from someone who's just a friend. I think I've known for a while I like Whinny more than Avery but being as stubborn and as stupid as I am I just had to give things a real shot with Avery. But I can't end things with her over the phone and now, so it'll have to wait. I go ahead and call her.

"Are you coming?" The words took me back to earlier after school when I asked her the same thing.

"Hello to you too." I say

"Yeah, yeah, so?"

"Well I was wondering if you wanted to go to Jacob's bonfire with me." I'm going to act as if nothing is wrong until I get the opportune moment.

"No."

"Why not?"

"I'm already in comfy clothes and want to be settled in for the evening."

"Yeah but by the time I get there you could already be changed and it's a Friday night so what do you say?"

"Michael just come here, why can't it just be us?"

I sigh "Avery I'm going to Jacob's, it's for seniors only and we're seniors."

"Fine"

"You went to the party on the roof with Lance."

"Yeah and I hated every minute of it. I went to see who you were going with."

"And now you don't want to be the one going with me?" Seriously that makes no sense.

"Maybe another time."

"Alright, night."

"Goodnight." She clicks off. I know she's pissed, but oh well. I walk out onto the field and sure enough Kevin's sitting in the center still dressed in his uniform.

"Hey man."

"Can you believe this is our last year here? I mean from freshmen year and all the shit we were given, all the tough, grueling work outs, and sometimes three a day to just a few more weeks left here on this field." He looks up at me. Kevin usually only talks about serious stuff with me, but I'm sure that's because out of all of us, we've been the friends the longest. He's like my second brother and really helped me when I lost my real one. I sit down beside him.

"Crazy huh?"

"I know this is kind of far off yet but have you picked out a school?"

I think heavily before responding. "Not really, you?"

"Nah, Tennessee looks good, but so do a few small schools. Hell I may even stay here and do community college and try to get on coaching here."

"No way man, you're better than that, you need to be playing."

"I've got time to decide I guess; I just feel like it's ticking way to fast."

"You've got time dude. I haven't decided yet either. Who knows, maybe in class inspiration will hit you." Then I laugh.

"Who told you that line of cheesy crap?"

"Whinny."

"God bless her. She really is the sweetest. I've had study hall with her the all four years of high school. She's unique in the best way possible. Man she took a hard hit tonight too and she doesn't even play football." We both laugh. I know we shouldn't joke about what happened, it could have been a lot worse. Hell maybe it even is. She never came back to cheer in the fourth quarter, at least I don't think she did.

"She can handle it, she's tough."

I usually don't ask any of the guys anything about their personal lives, but right now I do. "Do you talk to your dad about college?"

"Yeah, he gives pretty good advice, I probably listen to his advice more than I do my mom's" Kevin smiles "he likes to tell stories from when he went."

"I wish I had that right now. I wish I had a backbone, someone else to just tell me everything's going to be alright and it'll all work its self out. You can only tell yourself for so long before it feels fake. And mom she's just not here. I didn't even have dinner with her once this past week. She was out almost every night until 10 and she won't tell me what she's doing. Sometimes she'll come home then say she has to go to the store or forgot something at work. I can't describe it. I've tried talking to her and telling her I need her, but instead of reaching out to me as an adult she just launches into these old lectures that do no good." Kevin's listening intently to me. "You asked what was up with Whinny, and I can't tell you because I don't even know. But she's been the only person who I've really talked to about college and we really didn't get very far into the conversation. She's the only person who's told me everything is okay and that no matter what I chose it should be from the heart and I won't go wrong."

"Sounds to me like she might be that backbone you need."

"How could I have not noticed her until now? I mean we live next door to each other."

"No offense, you've always been a great friend, but while you and Jasmine were together, you really didn't see much else. The only things we ever talked about were football, or her."

"I was really that shallow huh?"

Kevin laughs "you aren't shallow, you weren't shallow, you just didn't care about anything else. You had the good looking girl and that's all that mattered to you."

"How am I now?"

"You're better, you've changed, but I don't think it was just because of your breakup. I know this past year has been hard on you. Now you think about every little thing and how you can stand up and be the man in every situation, you feel like you need to fix everything and now you think about things differently." I stare straight ahead.

"Maybe"

"Michael, relax, you're not a superhero and no expects you to be. Just concentrate on yourself. I promise as a friend; I won't let you fail."

"Thanks buddy" I smack him on the shoulder.

"Come on, let's get to Jacob's and not think about college."

"I could go for that." I know we shouldn't be concentrating on college this hard this early into the year but it's kind of hard not to when some classmates have already decided on a school and have declared their majors.

Almost all the seniors are out at Jacobs. It's cool that no one invited the juniors, sophomores or freshmen. I happen to be wondering about Whinny. They acted as if everything was fine and that she would be back by the end of the game, although I didn't see her. But then again the game was starting to pick up and get intense. I was pretty in the zone, so maybe she did come back.

Someone changes the iPod song and everyone whoops and hollers running closer to the sound system to dance their asses off.

"About time you two love birds show up." Lance and Shane dance up to us.

"Come on loosen up, we just won our second game, and a conference game at that."

"Victory is ours!" Shane shouts and everyone goes crazy and shouts the same thing back. Our school is really big into football. Shane takes another drink, I know that some of the guys are drinking, I just hope not too much. Jasmine spots me and is walking this way, all the cheerleaders still in their uniforms.

"Great game Michael" She throws her arms around me.

"Thanks." I can smell the alcohol on her breath.

"Where's Avery? Mr. I don't want a girlfriend."

"I don't know."

"Probably out with another guy getting an S.T.D." She smirks. She has definitely already had too much. I'm glad Lance has already walked away.

"Say what you want Jasmine but at the end of the night she's still the one with me." At least for a few more hours. I give her a nice smile, pull her arms away and walk away leaving her standing there with her jaw dropped. I do have to admit though it seems weird to not be here with her. We always did these party type ordeal things together.

I walk around the fire smacking hands with people saying 'great game' 'good win' and 'congratulations' I stop where Joe and a girl from our class, Melissa are conversing.

"Awesome game Michael, another win to hopefully an undefeated season."

"Thanks Melissa." I smile; it's nice to have so many people backing us. All of a sudden I get bumped from behind by someone and turn to see who.

"I'm so sorry." Says the voice.

"Whinny?" She's here after all. I'm surprised, but who cares she's here. The music gets turned up and is loud, people start dancing around us and we're pushed close together.

"Michael!"

"You're here. How are you feeling?"

"Yeah but I have to work all day tomorrow and Sunday since I took this evening off. And okay, still a little hard to catch my breath and my body aches all over but overall I can't complain."

"That was a tough fall." I pull back to look at her face. I can tell something's not quite right. "You must be accident prone.'

"Ha, probably, and yes it was, but eventually I'll be okay. I'm actually lucky it could have been worse." She's trying so hard to muster up a strong profile. Then she says "I heard what you whispered in my ear." I look in her eyes, not really sure what to say. I mean it's not like I can just come out and tell her I have feelings for her. She gets pushed from behind and falls into my arms.

"You alright?" I say close to her ear. She lays her head on my chest for a second. It's the most comforting thing I have ever felt. Her face is scrunched up and she tears up. She's in a terrible amount of pain. She puts her hands against my ribs to push herself back up, well attempt to push herself back up, she's really weak all of a sudden. When she looks up at me and our eyes meet I feel my breath catch. Here in this moment I want to kiss her.

I think she feels it too because suddenly she looks away and says "I'm good." I push her back up and help her regain balance then let go.

"Whinny, what's wrong, there's something you aren't telling me." She looks away as if trying to find an excuse to get out of this conversation. I take her tiny elbows and pull her closer to me.

"Whinny, I'm not letting you go until you tell me."

Finally, she looks into my eyes. Her eyes are watery. "Promise you won't tell anyone?"

"I promise."

"I'm serious, it can't get back to anybody on the cheerleading team or even my coach."

"I'm not going to tell."

"I have a broken rib, if anyone finds out they won't let me keep cheering and I can't afford not to cheer."

"You have to rest."

"Michael you said you wouldn't tell, please, I'm begging you." Her face reads she's scared and worried. "Michael." She whispers.

"Okay, I won't tell" But truth is, I'm worried. She's really going to hurt herself.

"Thank you." I let her go, it feels like the hardest thing I've ever had to do, besides watch my brother be put six feet down.

"Whinny what changed Monday?" She looks away again I can tell something's not right.

"Michael please, please stop with all the questions. I can't hurt you."

"There's nothing you can say or do that's going to hurt me, except keeping your distance. That might actually do more than hurt me. I know we haven't spent any time together in the past and every day now I regret it."

"Don't regret it Michael." She cuts me off "things might not be the way they are now if we'd known each other the whole time. I believe everything happens for a reason, both good and bad."

"But things really are different now Whinny and I meant what I said to you after you fell. I'm going to continue to hunt you down if you ignore me, so in the long run it'd just be easier for you to give in." She smiles a small smile.

"Fine."

"Fine seems like a pretty bland word." This time she laughs.

"Okay, I won't just up and disappear." She looks so small and fragile and cold and vulnerable and just everything. Or maybe that's just the way I see it because I want so badly to protect her. I never want any harm to come to this girl and it's because I am honestly just crazy about her.

"That's all I ask, and thank you in return."

"Well in that case can you do me a favor? Will you let me know when you leave? I think Jimmy's a little too intoxicated to be driving." I follow her gaze to where Jimmy's grinding on Katie.

"Of course."

"Thanks. I need space." She pushes her way out of the group of people that have surrounded us. I still think something's off with her but I'm not going to press the issue. I find my way out as well and head to the front porch of the cabin where Shane and Parker are sitting on the railing just watching everything. I climb up and sit with them.

"Crazy party huh?"

"I'd say, everyone is acting like they haven't been to a party in ages."

"Ha, school will do that to you, even though we had one last week."

"Hey how did that end anyways?" I ask

"It was okay. The janitor came up after about an hour and said it was time to shut it down. And if we didn't he'd get us all in trouble. So we did."

"So he knew his keys had been copied?"

"I don't think his nephew was too sneaky."

"It was still cool that it happened though."

"Yeah, I'm glad he told us to cool it. It could have been bad if we would have gotten caught."

We sit up here talking and watching most of the night. Mostly about the game then a little about our school assignments, followed by the girls in our class that have really seemed to change this year compared to last, both physically and in personalities.

I really can't believe I'm in such a good mood. But I'm with the other seniors and it feels right to be here, we won our game and Whinny is talking to me. I've tried finding her throughout the night but I haven't had much luck. I really hope she doesn't overdue things, a broken rib, that's a big deal. I'm kind of surprised her coach doesn't know since she ended up having to go to the hospital. But it's not my place or my business.

It's going on one and I'm definitely starting to feel tired. I don't want to drag Whinny away from here considering she's always working and never gets to do any extracurricular activities, and on account of she's had a pretty rough night. Thankfully I see her walking towards Shane, Parker, myself and Kevin who joined us maybe an hour ago. She looks rough, just physically beat up but makes sense as to why.

"Jimmy is staying the night, so thankfully I don't have to worry about him."

"How's he feeling after taking that tackle?" Kevin asks

"I guess fine, he hasn't said too much about it, just "see that's why I never wanted to play football. Who wants another guy's sweat all over them anyways?" She says the last part in a guy's voice and all us guys kind of get a kick out of it. Whinny's pretty much a character, but you'd never know unless you take the time to get to know and talk to her.

I had gotten a chance to ask Kevin what Whinny is like, since they've had study hall together all of high school. He said she's always helping others and making the room feel lighter. He said she's just a good hearted person. I feel extra lucky that I've been given a second chance to get to know her.

"Well more importantly how are you feeling?"

She sighs "I'm okay, it was scary. I've learned to put so much trust into Jimmy and our partnership. All of a sudden he wasn't there, my heart stopped. But overall really I'm good. Thanks for asking." Kevin smiles at Whinny. Parker jumps off the railing and puts his arm around her waist. She grimaces slightly but quickly smiles again.

"I'm pretty sure every guy wishes all girls could be as hot but yet understanding and nice as you." I can't help but feel intense jealousy. I wish he'd take his hands off her.

"I'm pretty sure you're wrong, but thank you."

"Let's be honest, would you ever consider dating me?"

She smiles "Parker, you know you don't date girls."

"What's that supposed to mean?" She raises her eyebrows at him. "Come on baby, you know that's not true. I've had a four-month relationship before."

"Michael are you ready?" Whinny turns her head quickly towards me.

"Very much so." I jump off the railing, more than eager to get her out of Parker's grip.

"You never answered my question." Parker pulls her back into him, real close and she lets out a gasp.

"Parker, easy."

"Michael, I'm just talking to the pretty lady." He squeezes her again and spins around so he's standing in between Whinny and I. Still with his hand around her. Whinny's face scrunches up.

"Parker, she's sore and you're hurting her." Parker has had a little too much tonight. I step over and pry his hand from her waist, glad he doesn't try and stop me again. I put my hand on her back and direct her in the direction of my truck. "Don't drive tonight." I tell him. I look at the other guys and they know too not to let him drive.

"See you guys Monday." Kevin and Shane will leave soon I have a feeling but they were really getting a kick out of watching everyone. When people get obliterated they tend to make complete asses out of themselves and there is plenty of that going on tonight, even Parker had more than he should have.

Whinny stops at Jimmy's mustang to get her bag. I have to admit Whinny is in great shape, she's still in her uniform which is showing off much defined four pack abs and athletic toned legs that look like they could be a models. I take the bag from her. She gives me a look but doesn't say anything.

"So are you glad you made it?" I ask as we climb in my truck, I notice it's a struggle for her. I turn the engine over.

Whinny smiles "Yes I am; it was a lot of fun. Was the roof party this much fun too?"

"I guess, probably not as great though. I guess after an hour the janitor came up and told them they needed to shut it down. The guys seemed okay with it, none of us can afford to get into trouble."

"Touché" We make it off the rock driveway and turn onto the main road. "Thanks for the ride home. Jimmy promised he wasn't going to drink, go freaking figure."

"Maybe he felt tonight was stressful. But seriously no problem, you know Whinny I don't mind giving you rides. We do live right next door to each other."

"Yeah well you minded when you were sixteen so sorry if that era sticks with me a little more than this current one." I feel like I just got punched in the stomach. I really was an ass to Whinny, I don't even deserve for her to give me a chance, and then she sighs. "I'm sorry about Monday. I didn't mean to be so rude, but now that you're with Avery I feel like we should keep our distance."

"Whinny it's not the end of the world for us to hang out and besides Avery is a very understanding, non-jealous type of person." Once again I feel my words are tighter than necessary. I want so badly to tell Whinny how I feel.

"You're right, that's why I feel bad about me being mad at you."

"I forgive you."

"Phew, what a relief"

"Oh shut it, smartass. But remember you promised you won't disappear anymore" She laughs and I smile.

"Well speaking of Avery, why isn't she here?"

"Long story, I'd rather not talk about it."

"Are you guys okay?"

"Yeah" Whinny gets that I really don't want to talk about it.

"You know; this is new to me too."

"What is?" I ask

"Being friends with you. It's like one day out of the blue we decide to hang out and ever since we've been friends. It just happened so fast. And not at all what I was expecting."

I smile to myself in the dark. "Well what were you expecting?"

"That after the night of the movie I wouldn't talk to you again. I figured it was a one-time ordeal because you wanted to take your mind off something. That you only asked me over to be a distraction, that's why I took so long to say yes. I finally agreed because I actually wanted a distraction myself. But then the next night you came over and were all upset about my eye and boom here we are. Friends."

"So if I wouldn't have come over that night, you probably wouldn't have talked to me again?"

"Honestly, probably not. We've never been in the same group of people; we've never had the same friends. We've gone different courses."

"Well in that case, I'm beyond glad I did, because I like it. I know you probably hate my guts for how I treated you over the past couple years, but I really like where we're at now. I'm glad we didn't completely miss this opportunity."

"I don't hate you. It's not like you threw rotten eggs at me." She stops before saying, "but I do too" She sinks down and leans her head against the back of the seat. We drive for about five minutes in silence. Rain starts lightly beating down on the top of the roof and my window. For some reason I want to ask Whinny about her childhood after me and my brother stopped talking to her. I want to get to know her on a deeper level.

"Whinny?" No response, I glance over and notice that she's fallen into the window and is sleeping. I slow down with the rain which has picked up and for the fact that I've approached town. I feel good that Whinny is comfortable enough with me to fall asleep while I drive. Some people really have issues with getting into vehicles with others. Not that I can say I blame them, it's scary to know your life is in someone else's hands.

I'm hoping this rain carries over into tomorrow and I might not have to work. I feel for Whinny that that's all she really does, but at least she got out tonight.

I pull into my driveway, the rain beating down heavier than before. We need this rain badly. I turn my truck off and sit a minute, Whinny doesn't budge, she must really be out. I don't know if I should wake her or let her sleep. I check my cell phone, no new messages from Avery. I wonder how far in the hole I am after tonight, guess it really doesn't matter. I sit thinking about this past summer and Avery and I. Like the things that attract me to her, and how we could talk forever without having anything to talk about. Now I wasn't interested in those conversations, now I wasn't interested in her. Everything seemed so easy over the summer, so why was us actually dating so much harder? I'm guessing actually being back in school. Now all my time and attention is on football and not her. Maybe because I met someone else. It's crazy to think how quickly things and feelings can change. You think everything is great then one day, one person later everything changes. I'm guessing part of that is also due to the fact that I've never really liked Avery as much as I thought I did.

Next thing I know I wake up leaning against my truck window. Whinny's still sleeping as well, leaning against the passenger window, only she's all curled up in my football sweatshirt. It has our school name and football team on front with our last names and numbers on back. She must have gotten cold sometime during the night. I check my clock which reads seven thirty.

"Whinny." I nudge her arm.

"What?" she says sleepily.

"I don't know what time you're supposed to be at work…"

She jolts up "Oww, Crap!" She grabs her side "Damn that hurt. I got to go." She opens the door and jumps out. "Thanks Michael." I watch as she runs awkwardly to her house, it's still raining but only lightly. I call work while sitting here. They tell me to come in at noon, damn. I finally decide to make my way inside.

"You were out all night!" Mom freaks.

"No, I fell asleep in my truck in the driveway."

"What? You couldn't walk the twenty feet to come inside and sleep on the couch? Gosh Michael you could have said something!"

"I'm going to be on my own next year mom."

"Yeah, well last time I checked you still live under my roof!" She snaps.

I step back "alright, I'm sorry." Then I feel mad "no actually I'm not. Mom I respect you but every night this past week and the week before you were out till ten or later, please do explain that to me?"

I've never seen mom glare at anyone as hard as she is with me right now. "Michael Roy Statemen." She says through gritted teeth.

"Well it's true, I've tried telling you that I need you in my life, I need you at football games and I need you to be here for freaking dinner every now and then. I still need some guidance from you. But you won't talk to me. I feel like everyone in my family has abandoned me. And that's hard to deal with knowing I have some huge decisions to make this year and I feel like I'm making them alone. But I won't apologize for you not being around and me living me life. Yes, I stayed all night in the driveway, but until you step up to the plate and start acting like my mom again I think it should be okay for me to do such things."

Her jaw drops. I turn and head upstairs. I'm aware that I could be severely punished for what I just said, but maybe just maybe I finally got through to her.

Chapter Eight

I start at twelve and finish at six. I push mowed four lawns and walked Mrs. Rain's dog again. She tips well for that at least. I got rained on; I get in my truck and reach for my sweatshirt. It's not here and I remember that Whinny was wearing it when she dashed inside this morning. Actually sitting in the middle of my truck seat is still her gym bag. I check my phone, no messages or missed calls from Avery. I give her a call.

"Hey" I say when I hear her pick up.

"Oh so you do remember I'm your girlfriend."

"Well you really haven't done anything to make me think I'm your boyfriend."

"Whatever." She hangs up on me. I really don't want to fight with her. I'm a calm laid back kind of guy. I hate drama and fighting, yet it seems the only two girls I've been with have been that, all drama and fights. I feel like I can't do anything right without them getting mad. I call her back right away and I'm glad she answers, we need to go out tonight so I can hopefully break things off, peacefully.

"Avery let's go out to dinner."

"Fine, pick me up at seven."

"You pick the place."

"I will." She hangs up again.

I'm really scared to actually go inside once I'm home. Mom never said anything to me when I left for work. She's pretty much like a ticking time bomb, but then again right now I kind of feel like I am too. Once inside I smell food, mom's cooking.

"What's this for?" I ask cautiously walking into the kitchen

"Us. I think we need to have a conversation."

"Mom, I'm sorry for earlier."

"I guess some of it was true." Her tone is flat. I know she's not happy with me.

"I do want to talk, but I'm going out with Avery for dinner, we need some us time apparently."

Surprisingly mom's tone lightens. "Oh, you're still with Avery? I thought there was another girl involved. I'm glad there's not, you two seem great together." I don't' say anything. Mom seems exceptionally happy I'm with Avery. What the heck? But instead I waste no more time in getting ready. I take a fast shower, and change into a button down and jeans. My hair is still wet when I leave. I end up getting to Avery's around seven ten.

"Sorry I'm late; Mom wanted to talk. I got out of there as fast as I could."

"I would like to eat at the Frying Pan."

"Really, you don't want to go anywhere nicer?"

"No thank you. The Frying Pan is a quaint place to eat." Avery pulls her hair over one shoulder. We get in my truck and I back us out of her driveway, we ride in silence the whole way. We get there and head inside. Jamie who's a junior at our school is the hostess and seats us. I wonder why Avery wanted to come here. And then as I start to pick up the menu I see the reason why, at least I think that's why. Whinny has her hair piled on top of her head in a kinky bun like she did the evening we first hung out; she has on a black quarter length polo and a khaki skirt. No way, surely she wasn't the reason Avery wanted to come here, I think to myself as Whinny approaches.

"Hey guys, welcome to the Frying Pan, have you had a chance to look at our menus and see what you would like to drink?"

"Water with lemon, extra ice" Avery glares at me the whole time.

"Dr. Pepper for me."

"Alright, I'll be back in just a minute." I look at Avery once Whinny's gone.

"Really?"

"What? You don't like her waiting on us, it's her job Michael." She put emphases on waiting and job.

"Hey Michael, great game the last night." Mr. Jenkins says walking out with his wife and kids.

"Thank you, hope you come out to our next home game."

"We plan on it." I turn my attention back to Avery.

"What's that supposed to mean? At least she has a job and is working."

"Oh so you're going to stick up for her? I'm just some lazy bum."

"I never said that, I know you're busy with school and I am not sticking up for her, you're the one making it seem like it's a crime to be a waitress."

"No I'm not, but admit you're sticking up for her."

"Avery, I am not."

"Really Michael, you don't want to claim up to anything?"

"What?" I feel exhausted.

"Because you two looked pretty cozy last night." She stares at me for a minute before pulling out her cell phone and showing me a picture of Whinny and I leaning in really close to each other talking, my hands on both her elbows. It was when I was talking in her ear but the picture almost makes it look like I'm giving her a kiss.

"The music was loud so we were leaning in to talk to each other. It was a two-minute conversation and that was the only time we were together." Whinny comes back with our drinks; I notice she's moving stiffly. I feel bad, I want to do something to help her but I can't.

"Have you guys looked over the menu or do you need more time?" Avery and I are in the middle of a staring contest. "I'm going to go with you need more time." Whinny walks off.

"That's not what someone else said."

"Oh yeah I drove her home. Jimmy was supposed to drive her but he was way too drunk. He ended up spending the night." I sit back in my chair thinking. Avery has always been understanding and forgiving, I've never pegged her to be a jealous type. However, with the way she's acting it'll make ending things much easier.

"Michael, you better be ready for this week's game. No distractions." The governor of our town approaches me and gives me a handshake.

"Mr. London I am very ready."

"We expect such great things for you guys this year."

"So do we, sir."

"Whinny how are you doing after last night?" The governor stops Whinny as she's walking by.

"Pretty good, I'm very lucky after a fall like that."

"Good, good, we all love watching you cheer. And Michael it was so nice of you to go check on her and help her up. You two make quite a pair." He smacks her on the back. "Great service tonight too. We love coming here. Goodnight."

"Night" Whinny and I say at the same time.

"Oh." She says as a whisper almost. She has tears in her eyes within an instant and is holding her breath. My heart goes out to her. I want desperately to say something, but I can't with Avery sitting here. Ahh the hell with it.

"Are you okay?" I finally ask her.

She just nods her head "I just need a second" then finally she stands up straight and walks with her trey of food to a table. I look back to Avery. She's getting beyond pissed at all the interruptions.

"I guess I missed quite a show last night, both at the party and at the game."

"Some of the cheerleaders got tackled during the middle of build and Whinny was dropped. They took her to the hospital, that's all."

Avery rolls her eyes. "When she comes back you are going to order for me. I want a chicken salad with extra cucumbers and ranch dressing on the side." I nod my head as Whinny returns. Wow she's sounding just as demanding as Jasmine used to be.

"Anything looking appetizing yet?"

"Uh yeah, she'll have a chicken salad, extra cucumbers please."

"And" Avery snaps.

"Oh ranch dressing on the side."

"And for you Michael?"

"Nothing" Avery shoots me a look from across the table.

"You are not going to sit here and watch me eat, order something Michael." I all of a sudden am not feeling the greatest and I don't think putting food into my system is going to help much. Whinny can tell something is going on, I know just by her facial expression and posture. Huh maybe her great 'reading people' technique is starting to rub off on me. I know she can usually read me like a book anyways. She says she can read everyone but I'm not so sure about that, I think it's just me.

"Oh miss, um Whinny." Someone from another table calls.

"I'll be right back, looks like you could use a few more minutes."

"Michael, get over yourself! I'm the one who should be mad at you. It's like you were basically cheating on me!"

"I'm sorry Avery! I had no thoughts about cheating on you. I've never been that type of guy and after this summer I'm surprised you didn't pick up on that. I thought you could trust me." Okay, I guess I lied. I did think about kissing Whinny and I wanted to, but I didn't and I really never would cheat on anyone.

"I thought I could, but you don't act like you want to be with me unless I'm pushing you." I sigh. She's right. What we had this summer was great. But I really don't want it and truth be told it's gone. I don't want her. I just got jealous when another guy did I was being completely selfish and hurting others in my process.

"You're right; I haven't been very fair to you. I'm not use to being with someone who's from an opposite click or who doesn't support the one thing I love the most. You realize I have everything riding on this, that I'm being offered football scholarships to all sorts of schools. So yes I'm mainly thinking about football. Avery this isn't something that is going to go away. I plan on playing in college. It's hard not to be able to talk to you about this when it's my life; it's my love and passion. And let's be honest I don't really relate to anything you like or want to do. We really just don't have anything in common." She's just glaring at me. "And Whinny's my friend, out of all people I thought you would be the one to understand."

"She wasn't before school started Michael, so from a girl's perspective it throws up a huge red flag."

"I never thought of it that way and I'm very sorry for making you feel that way, but really she's just a friend." We sit here in silence for about five minutes. Whinny comes back with Avery's salad, ranch on the side and all.

"Here Michael" She puts a plate down in front of me with a piece of cherry cheesecake on it. "It's on the house, helps settles the nerves. Now is there anything else I can get for you two? How's the salad look Avery?" For the first time all night Avery looks at Whinny and Whinny smiles. "You know there's no competition, and even if there was, you would win by a long shot. Jealousy is a cruel thing, you're better than that." Whinny slowly walks away, leaving both Avery and I speechless. If only Whinny knew that I really had feelings for her, she won me over.

The rest of dinner is still awkward and quiet. Whinny came back and did our refills and checked in with us. She seemed so confident with herself. I could tell Avery did not like being put in her place. I have a feeling Avery knows what's coming when we get back to her house but she hasn't said anything to make the first move so maybe she doesn't. I leave a tip and we head up front to pay Jamie. Avery wastes no time and heads out to the truck. I'm actually kind of embarrassed by her behavior.

"Was dinner up to your expectations this evening?"

"Jamie it's just me."

"Yeah, well we're supposed to be friendly and courteous to everyone. Not just the football stars." She smiles.

"I see, but yes it was great and the service was good too."

"That's good, we only have two waitresses this evening and one's pregnant so most tables are falling on Whinny." I glance back to see Whinny cleaning off some tables. She's in pain it's easy to tell.

"Ah, well thanks Jamie. Oh and charge me for a piece of cheesecake. Whinny brought me one."

"I know, and it's on the house Michael."

"Fine, I see how it is. You two are ganging up on me."

"Pretty much" She hands me my change. "Have a good rest of your evening."

"Keep it, actually give to Whinny. Night." I head outside where Avery's standing next to my truck.

"Michael you played really well last night. We're hoping for another win this Friday, and then we can have a pep rally." Three girls from our school are walking into the restaurant.

"Thanks and we plan on winning so you better plan a pep rally." They all giggle.

"Will do."

"Can you please unlock the truck; I'd like to get in." Avery says after the girls walk off.

"Sorry Jamie and I got to talking."

"Yeah it seems like everyone has something they want to say to you."

"Small town Avery."

"No shit, I can't wait to get out." We drive back to Avery's in silence. This is the first time Avery and I went anywhere in public, it didn't go so well. I pull in her driveway and shut the truck off.

"Avery?"

"What, you're not going to walk me to the door?" She starts to get out so I do too and follow her to the front door.

"What happened to us and this summer?" She finally stops trying to unlock the door.

"Nothing happened to us Michael, school started and now you're busy that's all, we're fine."

"Apparently not, you haven't smiled all night."

"Sorry I guess I'm back in school mood where we hate each other."

"You're the one who wanted everyone to know." She looks at me.

"I thought if we were together people would back off, you know, 'oh Michaels got a girlfriend we should respect that' I mean they all did when you and Jasmine were together."

"It's not like they don't know, but let's face it you're never around so how would they? You're not there for me to show off, or for you to stand up for me. So people are going to make a move. It's high school."

"I was tonight."

"Avery people were just congratulating me on the game last night."

"Well it was annoying considering they could tell we were trying to have a date. I don't like people in general and all the attention you get."

"So it's kind of like what I said before we started dating, we just like sneaking around, don't really want people knowing." She looks hurt.

"Yeah I guess."

"Avery I think we both know we'd be better off not dating. I just don't think we're ready. Not yet anyways, and to be honest we really don't have anything in common. I think I was just following my mind and memories from this summer."

"Yeah." She sniffles back tears.

"Thank you for a great summer though."

"Whatever." She walks inside and slams the door in my face. I stand here for a second wondering if ending things with Avery is the right thing to do. I miss her. But my hearts not in it so yes it's the right thing to do.

I drive home slowly thinking about Avery and I. I really just can't do this. I can't argue with anyone, A that's not healthy and B I put up with that for so long with Jasmine. I want to be free of drama. I want to just enjoy senior year. I should have never dragged Avery away from Lance, but then again I didn't know she wouldn't want to do anything with me or be so possessive. Also I didn't know my feelings for Whinny would escalate so quickly. I just need to worry about myself and get through this year. Like mom says "concentrate on all those scholarships." I think I just used Avery as a distraction after Jasmine and I broke up, but I'm not sure I ever had feelings, strong real feelings for her.

I arrive at home and look at Whinny's house, my heart beat speeds up. Damn it. Once inside my own home I find a note from mom. It says "going to the movies with Kelly, Love you." I go upstairs and fall asleep still in my nice clothes.

I wake up at seven thirty, change into some running clothes and head outside. I'm not much of a runner, I mean I do track, but the distance running isn't really my thing. But today I need this. As I'm running I make my way down by the ocean. It's a beautiful late

August morning. I stop to just watch the seagulls out over the bay. I begin to think which seems to be the only thing I do these days. The only time I'm not thinking is when I'm on the football field which in a way is slightly ironic.

I start up again and actually stop at my brothers' grave. I haven't been here since the day we buried him. Honestly when I need to talk to him or think about things I go to the tree house, but for some reason I felt the need to see his tomb. The thought that he's really gone still hasn't sunk in yet. Part of me feels like he's away at college having the time of his life and he hasn't gotten a chance to call yet. He was my best friend, even when we hated each other; we still were always on each other's side. We only had a year in a half between us; we even hung out with the same crowd when we were in school. It just doesn't seem real. At times I turn to talk to him and he's just not there, and that hasn't really hit home for me yet. And in a weird way sometimes I feel like he's trying to communicate with me through Whinny. I think he made us meet up and changed my current path. What are the odds that I had a feeling something was wrong with her and when I went to check those feelings were right? What are the odds that if I wouldn't have gone over there that night, that she wouldn't be in my life right now? I don't think it's fate, I think it's Max.

I sit down in front of his tomb. Then there's the fact that my dad left me and mom. He just couldn't handle being around here after what happened. He never stopped to think how his decision would affect me. I need to step up to the plate and be the man around the house; it's kind of hard to do when I myself am scared of the future. What if I don't get all the great scholarships mom is hoping for, what if I do, can I really leave her behind? What if I get the scholarships I really want but mom doesn't want me to go that far away for school? Will I regret not going to the best school I possibly could just so I can watch over her? After all it's my future. I'm the one who has to get up and do what's best for me, not what's best for us. And why won't mom talk to me right now? I know something has got to be going on she's so far out there, she's so far gone. How do I bring her back? How do I get her to realize I'm still here and will be for almost a whole year yet? And as corny as it sounds I still need her to be my mom.

I touch his tomb. "Thank you." I whisper before standing.

I start running again, taking the long way back towards home. I guess the only way to feel better about some of this, is to actually tell someone. I can't carry all this stuff on my own, but trying to catch Whinny is difficult. Maybe mom will be home, it is a Sunday. When I get back home, Avery's sitting on my front porch.

"Hey." I keep my distance and try to catch my breath.

"I'm so sorry Michael."

"Uh." I stand with my hands on my hips. For some reason I can't make myself approach her.

"I really like you. And I was a complete ass. I watched Jasmine boss you around for so long and all of a sudden I thought I could do that to you too. That's not me."

I don't know what to say. She gets up and starts walking towards me. "I feel really bad about last night. You don't deserve that."

"Thanks I guess. But after that remark about Jasmine pushing me around, ouch." I never realized until after Jas and I broke up that I was pretty much her bitch, and that feeling sucks, really takes away from the manhood thing.

"You're a great guy and you deserve a great girl. You deserve to be with someone who realizes you're the good guy, the genuine type, someone who doesn't take that for granite. All the girls in the school want to be with you Michael just don't let them treat you like Jasmine and I did."

"Uh. Okay." I'm not really sure where she's going with all this....

"I just wanted to come and apologize for my rude behavior. And even though I like you, I think you're right about us not having that much in common. Our personalities just don't mesh that well together. I'm going to talk to Lance and see if he'll forgive me. I'm not saying we'll date or anything, hell maybe not even this year, but I think he and I will have a better chance."

I smile at her. "Thanks Avery, there's the girl I met over the summer." She laughs and comes over to give me a hug.

"Eww sweaty."

"Yeah, my bad. You know, I'm glad we at least tried. We now know it just isn't going to work."

"I'm glad too." She pulls away. "Hey Michael?"

"Yes."

"I know a little bit more about Whinny than you'd think. She's a great girl, but she's been through a lot so be gentle."

"Umm. I don't really"

She cuts me off before I finish "Oh come on." She playfully bats my arm. "It's easy to tell there's something there. I'm not saying you two have to date, but the physical attraction is intense. I'm sure everyone could feel it last night." She laughs then says in a serious tone "I just know you care for her, but like I said, don't hurt her."

"I won't." Truth be told I'm more worried about her hurting me. I'm a little shocked at everything Avery's saying. "And I'm glad you're going to talk to Lance. He really likes you, and believe it or not, he's a good genuine guy too."

"I know. We've kind of been talking, even while we were technically "dating". Sorry about that."

"No harm no foul." We hug again. "So any chance you might tell me why Whinny is so fragile?"

"She'll tell you when she's ready. And I wouldn't say fragile is the best word."

"To be honest Avery, I really don't think I'm ready. I need to just be with myself, I have a lot of things I'm still trying to work through."

"I guess that makes sense. You did just come out of a pretty long relationship and have had a rough year."

"Wait, when were you close to Whinny and to know so much about her? She seems to keep to herself."

"You remember how we found each other on the beach?"

"Yeah"

"Well over the summer I'd go and watch the sunrise and Whinny and I met the same way. She was upset and seemed broken at the time so we talked. I've never seen her that way since. But we would meet up and hang out for about an hour almost every morning."

"You never told me that."

She shrugs her shoulders "I protect people I like. I knew she didn't want anyone to see her like that, so I never shared. Same thing as you and I, we're from different clicks. People would never guess that we're probably each other's best friends. We're still friends, even after last night. I know she'll forgive me. She knew I was out of line and was trying to put me back." Avery smiles.

"You really are a good friend and person Avery."

"Thanks."

All of a sudden Whinny comes flying out the door to her house with a duffel bag. There's a lot of screaming going on inside.

"I am NOT!" she yells before slamming the door. She comes off the porch and finally notices Avery and I. She quickly wipes away her tears.

"Are you okay?" Avery asks. Me, well I'm too stunned to say anything. Usually there's never a movement or peep coming from that house. Whinny hoists her bag higher on her shoulder, makes a face and starts walking towards the sidewalk.

"I'm fine, thanks for asking though." She has on regular clothes a tee shirt and jean shorts with her hair straight down. It's the first time I've ever seen her look regular, well I guess besides the first time we ever hung out.

"You should go after her." Avery touches my arm. "We'll stay in touch." She kisses my check and heads off in the opposite direction of Whinny. I watch as Whinny keeps walking. Why can't I just let her go? It's none of my business and I really shouldn't make it any of mine. But I need to see her. I jog and catch up with her.

"Where ya going?"

"Jimmy's. We're supposed to practice some new stunts."

"Whinny you can't, you fell yesterday! It's way too soon."

"They're simple stunts, I'll be fine." She's completely straight faced with me. She's still wiping some of her tears.

I sigh, "are you off today?"

"No, not all day." I reach out and grab her arm and turn her towards me, finally stopping her from walking.

"You want to talk?"

"No." I stare into her eyes and she just comes undone, sobbing heavy. I pull her in, her head on my chest, I wrap my arms around her. I finally get to see the human side of her, the side I saw the first night we hung out. I get to see the raw and emotional Whinny. The one who actually is vulnerable. We stand like this for about two minutes before she pulls back wiping away her tears. "Sorry."

"It's okay to let things out. I know I sure have."

She nods her head at me.

"Whinny I'm worried about you pushing things so hard and quickly, you need time to let your body heal."

"Okay, I promise I won't do anything stupid." I look at her, not sure if I believe her, I think she's just telling me what I want to hear, but I'm going to let it go. I switch topics completely hoping to help lighten the mood for her.

"Okay, then I want you to ask me something."

"What?" She draws back.

"The first time we hung out at my house I asked you a lot of questions supposedly. You never got your chance to ask me anything. So ask."

"Michael." She pushes me away "I need you to leave me alone." She turns and starts walking again. I smile a small smile and before I have time to really think about what I'm doing I catch up with her, grab her arm and pull her into a full embrace and hold her tight. I know I might be hurting her a bit but this way she knows she can't go anywhere. She doesn't fight or resist me. Finally, she lets her bag drop and wraps her arms around my waist.

"So are you going to ask me any questions?" I say after a minute.

She thinks a minute. "Do you consider yourself my friend?"

"Yes Whinny you're my friend; do you consider me one of yours?"

"Yes. Tell me what happened with Avery, last night was awkward."

"It was, we broke up. She came over to apologize for how rude she had been last night. And she told me she was going to try a relationship with Lance."

"Why Lance?" She asks to my chest.

"I'm sure you know. After all you two are best friends."

All of a sudden she pulls back hard, I wasn't expecting it and she breaks through my arms. "What did she tell you?" Fear is written all over her face.

"Nothing Whinny. Just that you two met over the summer and hung out a little bit. That's it. So I'm sure she told you about me and Lance." She looks relieved. Interesting. Whinny's got a deep dark secret that's she's afraid of. I wish I could help her through it and take all the pain away for her.

All of a sudden her demeanor changes. She's no longer feeling down, she actually seems more aggressive, in her expression and tone. "Okay, next question. Are you really over Jasmine?"

I cock my head to the side "very much so Whinny, I was ready to be out of that relationship before Prom last year. And I should have been. I should have stepped up and ended it sooner." I take a step closer to her. I really want to kiss her.

"Are you mad at me?"

"What? No, why? Should I be?" I step just a little bit closer to where now I'm standing over her looking down into her green eyes and she's looking up into my brown.

"Are you going to kiss me?" it comes out almost as a whisper.

"Yes." I reach my hand up and cup her neck pulling her a little closer and we kiss. It's the best kiss I've ever experienced. I can feel all of my body come alive, which might not be so great right now, after all I'm in gym shorts. When we finally pull apart I feel my stomach drop, and I actually feel sad? What the hell? She takes her hands and places them on my ribs as she leans her forehead against my chest.

"You really care about me don't you?" she asks, her voice quivers holding back tears.

"You're really all over the place with these questions aren't you?" I laugh "But yes Whinny, I do. I've felt something the minute you walked over and asked me to get your kitten out of the tree. I've never fallen for anybody before with just a look and a simple conversation, but I did for you."

"I've never had anybody care for me before."

"That's not true, your parent's do."

"No Michael I ha…" she stops midsentence. "Not the way yours care for you. And my kittens gone. Dad found out about him and took him." The whole time she talks she keeps her head against my chest. I wrap my arms around her again, lightly this time.

"I'm so sorry."

"I don't want to talk about it anymore" She finally pulls back and I let her go, she wipes away her tears. She turns around and sobs some. I put my hand on her back.

"Let me help you, talk to me." She turns back around.

"You don't get it, Michael. I want to, but right now I can't. I'm okay, you just have to trust me."

Hearing she can't hurt me, but I also understand how right now might not be the best timing. "Alright, well what do you think is going to happen between us?" I ask

"I don't know."

"Well do you care about me?"

"Michael." She smiles "I've had a crush on you since we were eight. I've watched the things you've gone through and how amazing you are, which has only made me like you even more. That's why I wanted to keep our distance after I found out about you and Avery. The more we talked the more you showed signs of caring, I was falling harder. And right now just, I don't know." Her cell phone rings and she answers. "I'm on my way. Yeah sorry parents were holding me up. About twenty minutes. Okay see ya." She looks at me. "I've got to get going."

"Whinny, please don't run from this."

"I just can't right now Michael."

"Please don't make me get down on my knees and beg."

She just looks at me. She starts to tear up again. "I'll see you sometime."

"Wait, Whinny."

"Michael, you probably just need some time to be single, explore your options. I don't think you know what you want. You know how I feel, you know I think very highly of you, but I need some space." She turns and keeps walking. I let her go. Damn. I bet I really messed this up. We've only been in school for two weeks and I've managed to ruin two friendships, well I guess one was patched, but seriously, how awesome am I?

Chapter Nine

It's now Wednesday and the beginning of September. Jasmine's been all over me since Avery changed her Facebook relationship status to single. Although I'll say Avery and I are much better off. The past few days at school have actually been easier than when we were "together", even if it was only a week. I haven't seen Whinny at all. I'm always worried something's going to happen to her as much as she walks and late at night. Also I know she's still in a lot of pain, a broken rib won't heal that quickly, she'll have a harder time taking care of herself if something would happen. She was going to be stunting with Jimmy and I'm afraid that didn't go very well. I know it sounds weird and just doesn't make that much sense, but just seeing Whinny makes me feel lighter. I need to figure out why every time we get close, she pushes back. She disappears.

I'm sitting in history, trying to concentrate on the notes, but I'm thinking about Whinny and the game Friday. It's our first away game. In the past we've always started out playing slow when we're away. I'm hoping that doesn't happen. Especially since I know there will be recruiters there. The University of Tennessee's head coach will be there, along with Alabama's head coach and even Old Miss is coming. I know they aren't coming just for me. We're going to be playing a 4A ranked number one school. They'll be there to see both teams. Coach informed me of this yesterday, and they'll be checking out Kevin too, but I can't tell him. Coach is afraid he won't play well if he knows.

The bell rings bringing me back to now. I gather up my books and head to my locker, inside is a note from Jasmine.

'You look super-hot today. I know you'll look this good when we take our picture for class cutest couple. Maybe we should work on the couple part again love jasmine' with a smiley face.

I wad it up and throw it away. I make my way into the cafeteria, get my food and finally sit down with all the guys. Well almost all, Lance isn't here. We talked on Monday and evened things out. I really am glad he's giving Avery a second chance. On an intellectual level they have so much more in common.

I look around at the cheerleaders table hoping I'll find Whinny. I don't see her.

"You guys will never guess what happened to me." Shane says.

"You won the lottery?"

"I wish. Keeley called me last night. I didn't answer."

"Wait, isn't she the psycho one from last year?"

"Yeah."

"Holy shit, she's back." Parker teases. Shane stands up, walks over to Parker and punches him in the arm.

"Ow, not cool."

"Neither is this, it wasn't a laughing matter last year and it isn't now either."

"You're right. Did she leave a voicemail sayin' what she wants?"

"Yeah, just that I should call her. What do you guys think I should do?" It surprises me that Shane's asking us for advice. I honestly wish I could talk to all the guys like that. Kevin and I have been friends since pre-school, and Lance and I became friends in first grade. Those are the only two that I ever actually 'talk to.' I met Joe in fourth grade, Parker in eighth and Shane freshman year during football.

"I think you should ignore her. She tried to ruin your life. She's finally out of it, best to keep it that way" Joe says.

"I think you should call her back and be honest with her." I realize I'm the one who just said that. I start thinking about how good it feels to have told Whinny I cared for her. I mean sure we aren't dating, but like she said at least we both know how the other one feels. "You should tell her its senior year and you're just concentrating on school and enjoying freedom." I continue. "I mean yeah she's bat shit crazy, but I think she deserves to know something, so give her something." All the guys are just staring at me.

"I think you're right Michael." Shane finally says. "I need to think about what I'm going to say." He instantly turns and heads out of the cafeteria.

"You think we should finish that music assignment?" Joe asks Parker.

"When's it due?"

"Duh, today."

"Oh shit, yeah." Parker slaps him on the arm "come on man, we got to go!"

"Later guys." They both pick up their treys and head out.

Kevin looks at me "you alright?"

"I think so, why?"

"You just seem kind of quiet this week."

"You've never really dated anyone, right?"

Kevin laughs "Yes and no. This summer I met a girl. It's been pretty hard to get her off my mind."

"What happened with her?"

"She was here vacationing, stayed a month then left. She was from Ohio and her whole family, including aunts, uncles and cousins made this trip. That's why they stayed so long. It would have never worked out, so I don't tell people about it."

"I'm sorry."

"That's life, sometimes things work out great and other times they don't."

"That's true. I wonder if I'll ever get to see you date someone." I look over at him with a stupid grin.

"Alright, what's going on?"

"Nothing."

He gives me this look. "Then why are bringing up woman?"

I laugh, "good question." I hesitate before saying "I stopped by Max's grave over the weekend, it was much harder than I thought it was going to be."

"I'm sorry dude. I really am."

"I wanted to tell mom about it, but Sunday she had a migraine and was in bed all day. Monday she was on the phone all night. Tuesday she was at cycle class and didn't come home until nine."

"You want to tell me about it?" I flash back to the day of the funeral and watching them burry Max. My heart aches in that moment. It was an open casket and I see the blank look on his face, a face that carried so much character. Growing up I had it all, an older brother, a mom and dad and now it's like I have nothing. Nothing but football and just some friends. I thought this year was supposed to be great, but right now it's hard.

"No. I just want to know you'll always have my back."

"Of course dude." He gets up, comes around the table and smacks my back. "We're brothers and you know that." I get up too. Time to move on with the day.

"Thanks."

"Alright Ladies" Coach yells. "I don't like calling you all ladies! So get out there, kick some ass and play hard. That way at the end of the game I can come in here and congratulate my MEN!" We all yell as we run out of the locker room, eager to get this game started.

The opening kick by the other team is deep. Alex catches it and heads up field getting tackled at the 37-yard line.

"Michael" coach grabs my jersey. "You want to make yourself look good, so play smart. The second play call is yours. Run red left lateral to start us off."

"We'll make you proud coach." I head out to the guys huddled up. "Alright let's do this. We're going to run red left lateral to Kevin."

"Break!"

"Blue 42, Red 29, Texas, Hike!" We march down the field and score a touchdown. My pass was a fast line drive to Kevin. I want to make sure he looks good this game too. The other team comes back the other way just as fast and scores a touchdown. It goes like this the whole game. Tied 21 to 21 we go into overtime. I stand in the middle of the huddle and look at each one of the guys. "This is our year! No mercy, no regrets! Break!"

"Sound one, sound two" defense does a switch, they're going to blitz, I change the play fast. "yellow, yellow," I quickly tell the offensive line.

"Bluebird on strike, 33, 34, 35 Hike!" I know our count offs are weird, but each one has a key word in it, to which the guys know which play to do. Yellow means a cut up, switch route and bluebird means mid field. So for us the tight end helps block on this paly and the two wide receivers run the route, starting to run down the sidelines then cutting back to the center or mid field.

I drop back looking around for my guys, nothing. I move out of pocket and take off running. Kevin seems to be the only one who heard, he's running along the left side line, me moving along the right. Now I'm waiting for the cut back. There it is with a fake step to the left he comes running toward me. Out of pocket and close to being pushed out of bounds, I plant my feet and throw the ball in front of Kevin downfield. I get tackled out of bounds. I look up in time to see him dive for the football into the end zone. Touchdown! What a hail Mary! What a catch! I get up and run to catch up with Kevin. We jump high at each other and do our usual touchdown routine. Game over and we win. Our fans go wild. I slap him on the helmet.

"Awesome catch, it's like you can read my mind."

"Awesome throw and I can. I'm your wide receiver, it's my job, plus we're bros!" What a great game for the recruiters to come and watch. Both teams have played our hearts out.

After we shake hands with the other team everyone gets ready to celebrate and fans and the cheerleaders start coming onto the field. Jasmine throws herself on me.

"Great game stud"

"Jasmine get off." She tries kissing me.

"Don't you want a good picture for the year book?"

"No, stop being so superficial"

"Michael, it's supposed to be you and me! I've given you some time, come on!"

"No, Jasmine I don't want "us" back." I'm finally free, afraid Whinny may have seen the show. I walk away and head back to be surrounded by more of my team, which seems to be heading into the locker room.

After I shower and change I emerge from the locker room and see Kevin talking to UT's head coach. Good for him. I've been talking to them too on the phone a couple times. It would be awesome if Kevin and I ended up going to the same school.

I find Whinny and head over to her as she's changing out of her cheering shoes. I haven't seen her all week, not even once. Not even before today's game. I stopped by her house to give her back the gym bag she'd left in my truck but she wasn't home so I left it with her parents.

"You know what? I think you won because I have your good luck charm." She says.

"And what is that?" She pulls out my football sweatshirt.

"I forgot you had that." She puts it on. "It looks good on you." Even though it's big.

"I think so too." She smiles. "Plus it's warm and cozy."

"Does that mean you aren't ready to give it back?" I sit down next to her.

"Do you want me to give it back?"

I smile "not really."

"Well we both agree it looks best on me, so maybe I should keep wearing it. Plus, I think y'all won because I had it."

"Oh… you don't think it had anything to do with us working our butts off?"

"Well." She leans her head against my shoulder. "Maybe a little." I smile. I can't believe how bad I want to be with this girl. But I can't figure her out. She tells me she likes me, but then she says I'm the one who needs space.

"How are you feeling? The rib getting any better yet?"

"I don't know. I hurt but I can at least do the stunts so no big deal. I go back in two weeks for another x-ray."

"You know I really think you should be taking it easy, if you don't give yourself time to heal you won't heal properly."

"I don't have time Michael."

"What, why not?"

I feel her smile, her head still on my shoulder. It's a pretty comforting feeling. "I have to do all these crazy stunts. All these new stunts are actually for college." She sits up and looks at me, her green eyes shining bright.

"College?"

"Jimmy and I have been given full ride scholarships if we can pull these off. The school that's giving us the scholarships is very challenging. But they love how much trust we already have in each other. Adding new lifts is nothing for us. They won't have to waste much time in training new people."

"Wow, Whinny that's awesome. So you and Jimmy are okay with going to the same college?"

"Not at first, but we both need the scholarships so we worked it out."

"I'm so happy for you." I lean in and give her a hug.

"Ow, Ow,"

"Sorry." I say, squeezing a little too hard. "So where are you guy's going?"

"Alright let's load up boys!" Coach hollers.

"Guess you'll find out another day."

"Just tell me real fast."

"Eh, I'd rather make you wait, means you'll have to come talk to me again someday."

I laugh, I really can't get enough of this girl. "I guess, but seriously that is awesome, I'm really happy for you."

"Are you ready Whinny?" Jimmy comes over and takes her bag. "Good game Michael."

"Thanks." I look at Whinny. She looks really small in my sweatshirt.

"See you?" I ask more as a question than a statement, because with her, I just really never know.

"Yeah" She gets up and heads with Jimmy to their bus. I can't believe how jealous I am of that guy. I try to tell myself to calm down. After all she's wearing MY sweatshirt.

Chapter Ten

It's been two weeks since our football game where all the recruiters came to watch. Kevin's phone has been ringing off the hook ever sense. I keep thinking how cool it would be if we would go to the same college and get to continue playing together, but I know it's a long shot. I don't think Kevin's as worried about going off to college now that he knows he'll have a scholarship wherever he wants to go.

Me, well I'm still having a hard time deciding. It's the middle of September and I know I've still got plenty of time but it's hard watching all the guys make decisions and then here's me who doesn't know top from bottom right now. In fact, the only person who makes me feel normal has been Whinny. She's been at school almost every day, for once. We usually meet in the library after second period and hang out in there. I'm honestly surprised how smart she is and how much school work she seems to know since she misses so much school. But spending that time with Whinny has now become my favorite part of the day and lunches with the guys my second favorite.

Even though we aren't in the same American History class we're working on a project together, but yet it has to be different so the teacher doesn't get too suspicious. Then after free period I walk Whinny to her locker. Then we head in opposite directions to fourth period then lunch.

"You know, I'm getting pretty use to this seeing and spending time with you during the day." I say today at her locker. She laughs.

"Yeah these past two weeks have been nice. But I don't really think you're getting the chance to explore your options."

"Whinny." I feel like she's going to run again. "You promised no more running away and disappearing." She closes her locker door. "Besides, I don't want time. I want you."

She bites her lip. "I didn't say I was. I'm just telling you that if you want freedom now's your chance." She gives me a wink. I don't say anything. Truth is even though Whinny and I aren't technically dating, we're still pretty much dating. I don't want freedom and time to explore options. I know she feels the say way so I can't understand why she won't give in. What's holding her back? She looks at her phone and I see her whole expression change. She's lost her playfulness. What could be happening when she reads those texts?

"I've got to get going. See you." She starts to head off.

"Whinny." She turns around. She looks like she's about to cry. "What's wrong?" I pull her in for a hug. She hugs me back then pulls away.

"Nothing, Michael I just need to get going. I'll see you tomorrow." She quickly leaves. I wish Whinny didn't have to go through this alone. I have no idea what "this" is, but I can tell it's getting to her. I really do want to be with this girl more than anything. I want her problems to be mine, I want her happiness to be mine. In all I just want her to be mine. I've just been trying to decide how I want to ask, I want it to be special, that's for sure.

Finally, I turn and head to History, before I get there Jasmine stops me. She's looking tan for September. She's wearing white jeans and a blue button down, still looking gorgeous as ever.

"What the hell?" She says

"Excuse me?"

"I don't understand why you won't give us another chance Michael. I mean first you go off and think Avery is going to fulfill your dying needs and now you're moving on to Whinny, please."

"Jasmine I told you a week after school started that we wouldn't be getting back together. It's not my fault you can't wrap your mind around that."

"No, what I can't wrap my mind around is you telling me that we are all going off to college in a few months so why bother getting tied down, yet here you are tying yourself to anything that has two legs and boobs."

I actually laugh "Whinny and I aren't dating Jas. I'm still single. And maybe I shouldn't have ever told you that, maybe I should have just been honest with you then and told you there was no chance of us ever again." She looks hurt. "I really need to get to class."

"I told you I've changed though and you dated me for almost 3 years and don't want to see if it's true?"

"Exactly. I know that sounds harsh, but there just aren't feelings here between us anymore and you and I both know there haven't been for a while. We were wasting our time. Who knows what will happen when we go off to college anyways, isn't it better to have ended it now." She shakes her head and a tear slides down her cheek.

"If you're going to end things when you go to college, then why do you keep wanting to date all these other girls?"

"Because I can. It's my life and my decision. It may be the right decision or it may be the wrong one, but it's still mine."

"Yeah, well I cheated on you. You didn't want to have sex with me, but everyone else did. I'm hot Michael, everyone wants me."

"Everyone except me. I'm sorry I held you back for so long." Her expression changes immediately. She thought she was going to hurt me and make me mad and jealous. It's her way of trying to get me back. It does hurt a little, actually a lot. Especially, when you think you know someone, but hey more power to the hoe. Then for some reason the night of sitting under the treehouse with Whinny pops into my mind. I can see her eyes and the look she gave me. I can't believe it. Whinny knew and never told me. She was the one protecting me.

"You cheated on me sophomore year with Ian." I say coolly. She cocks her head to the side. I can tell she's trying to decide if she should find a way to cover that up or just admit it. "Yeah, Jas I already know, but thanks for FINALLY being honest." Granite I wouldn't have known that if it wasn't for Whinny, but Jasmine doesn't need to know that. I'll just let her think I'm just that good. To be honest I don't feel sorry for me hearing this, I feel sorry for Whinny, and because of Jasmine she no longer trusts hardly anyone. Ian would have never stepped out on Whinny if it weren't for someone like Jas really pushing him.

"Michael, wait." She grabs my arm.

"Not going to happen, why would you even think it would after you tell me you cheated on me? Come one, you're not that stupid." I walk away, already ten minutes late for class. Hell I think I'll just skip it.

After practice I wait for Kevin to come into the locker room. I have a feeling he's going to take his sweet time leaving today. It was a long practice and an extremely hot one.

"Hey man." He says finally walking in and sticking his head under the shower and blasting the cold water.

"Hey."

"That feels good after today."

"Yeah, so have you heard Jasmine keeps trying to get back with me?"

"Ha, why when she's having so much fun being single?"

"I think just to prove me wrong."

"You know, I came into this year actually wanting to be in a relationship and football has just really taken over. Now that I'm in the zone, I want to stay there."

"Speaking of football, we haven't really talked about this yet, but you're going somewhere to play right?"

"Hell yeah. I don't want to stay around here, or at least not yet. I wouldn't mind coming back and raising my family here, but for now it's time to move on."

"Where ya think you're going?"

"I don't know." I can tell Kevin's not really in a talkative mood.

"Alright, well I'm out. I'll see you tomorrow."

"See ya." When I come out onto the field I see Whinny practicing all sorts of flips without using her hands. She keeps making terrible facial expressions. All that twisting has got to hurt. I wonder where she needs a ride to today. I wonder if everything's okay? She changed moods so fast today.

"You're pretty good at those, even while in pain." She's catching her breath. She may not admit it but her rib is still giving her fits. She walks over and picks up her phone. She stares at it for a few seconds while she catches her breath. Not that damn phone. I'm trying to read her expression but she's giving nothing away.

"Everything okay?' I ask. She looks at me then comes walking right up to me and kisses me. I let my duffel bag fall to the ground. I wrap one of my arms around her back and the other around her neck. It's a deep salty but sweet kiss, and a much unexpected one. It takes my breath away but leaving me wanting more. I feel like I can't get close enough to her. It's like time stands still. When we pull apart I feel lost and very aroused.

"I'm sorry, I just wanted to do that for a while now." She says, even though we have kissed before it was nothing like this and it's been a couple weeks.

"Don't be sorry, it's very much appreciated."

"I just don't know what to do with you Michael."

"Excuse me?"

"I don't think I can keep being friends with you, not when I feel the way I do. I don't want you to break my heart and I know you'll be the guy to do that."

"Whinny I don't plan to ever hurt you." I have no idea where any of this is coming from. Her phone???

"Yes you will, not intentionally but you will when our senior year is over and we both go off to separate colleges, being that far from you will break my heart."

"We don't necessarily have to go to different schools; I think you should tell me where you're going. At least then I'll know."

"I can't do that Michael. I won't have you choosing a school just because I did."

"Whinny please don't back away from us now. Please don't walk away. I want you in my life. I need you in my life." I see her look over at her duffel bag with the phone laying on top.

"I have too, I really am sorry. I'll always think of you." She starts towards the bleachers.

"Don't do this." I actually have tears in my eyes. She keeps walking and doesn't look back. "Whinny, please free fall with me." I pick up my bag and start after her. I can't let her go, if she leaves now, I'll never find her again. Kevin comes back out onto the field and runs up to me, stepping in front of me.

"Hey, Sorry I was being an ass in there; you wanted to talk about something?"

"No it's fine dude, I have to go."

"Alright but I'm still a good listener, and the smart one." I look at Kevin who's smiling.

"Kevin seriously give me a minute." I push past him and look at the bleachers. She's gone. I look everywhere but she's gone. And just as easily as Whinny walked into my life, she walked right back out.

"You alright Michael?" Kevin asks

"No."

Chapter Eleven

Finally, we've reached the end of our season. It's the last week of October and next weekend we start Sectional. We only lost one game this season, which is huge. Everyone's pretty hyped up about Sectionals. Most of us guys haven't started thinking about it yet. We're still trying to get through practices. Coach hasn't backed down on the training and most days we're still out practicing at six. Mom hasn't made it to any of my games, although she promises to come to Sectionals. She's gotten a little better these past two months, but I still think something's going on. She was very upset when she found out Avery and I weren't together anymore. But her mood lightened when I told her I'm single and just concentrating on football.

We never did have that conversation. We just kind of pretended that whole episode never existed. I guess I'm good at that though. She's still jumpy, always pale and buying new clothes all the time. She says her wardrobe lacks assertiveness and that she can't find the right "look." She won't talk to me about it though, she really won't talk about anything other than school and football, so I've just let it go. I have other things to worry about, like getting through this weekend.

Our school is having our fall dance. Lance and Avery are going together. They've been hanging out since the end of August, right after me and her, but they aren't officially dating yet. She hasn't come to a game yet either, but she also promises to be at Sectionals.

Parker has started dating Lucy. She's a junior and on the volleyball team, they just lost in the final game of Sectionals, at least she has another year. They're going to the dance together. Although most of us are surprised that Parker is actually with a girl. The rest of us are still single. I've tried to get Kevin to open up and talk about the girl from over the summer, but he won't bite at the bait. And he's tried getting me to open up about Whinny and what happened that day on the football field. I still don't even know what happened. Every time I'm with Whinny and she looks at her phone things go askew. In a weird way it's like someone has control over her and every time we start to get close they blow the whistle and in which she disappears. I made her promise not to do that to me again, but I guess that's hard to do when we weren't actually together. She still has my sweatshirt; she usually wears it to and from football games. Which makes Jasmine insanely jealous considering I never let her wear any of my clothes the whole time we dated. She's pretty much hated me ever since our talk in the school hallway.

I'm pretty crazy about Whinny. I haven't once stopped thinking about the day on the football field. She pretty much disappeared from my life. Occasionally I'd see her in the hallways and we'd talk but she's always been in a rush to get gone. About the deepest our conversation ever got was how's the weather? She stopped coming to the library with me and wouldn't be around for me to walk to her class. It's like everything we had had, just vanished. But not in a broke up kind of way. It's just like Whinny completely disappeared making me wonder if she was ever really here or was it all just my imagination.

I would even go over to her house during the week but her parents always covered for her, even when I knew she was there. I also would occasionally stop in at the Frying Pan. She never wanted to see me, or wasn't there. I was getting her message loud and clear, but what I really want is an answer as to why she flipped a switch. I've been dying to know what I need to do to get her back in my life. I know I should just give up and move on, but I can't. She's the only person who's made me feel like me again, since Max's passing. I didn't even realize I wasn't me until she came into my life. Everything then just became more clear and sound. I may be young but I also realize that's a feeling you don't find with everyone you meet. I can't just let that go.

She cheers at games but usually by the time I get out of the locker room she's already headed to the bus or gone. She got her x-rays back. She's apparently all healed and I guess Jimmy's already pushing to start stunting with flips again and she's agreed. That's pretty much all she told me yesterday when I saw her. Let's just say it's been a long month in a half without her. I've been pretty quiet and most of the guys have noticed but haven't said anything. I've been playing good games so why interfere with that. I've put all the thoughts of not having anyone at games to support me, out of my head. Because I no longer care, what I do care about is getting scholarships and in order to do so, I have to play well.

It's finally lunch though and I plan on finding Whinny, even if she's not in the Cafeteria, I'll hunt her down. I can't wait to ask her to the dance. I'm hoping no one else has asked her yet. Apparently there are a lot of guys who are really into her, even though she's like a ghost. And I know I should have asked her to go with me sooner, but since she's kind of been avoiding me, it's been a little hard. I'm fully aware her answer will probably be no, but I'm not taking that today. Today I plan on finally getting to the bottom of everything.

I head through the cafeteria doors and see Whinny over talking to Avery. I head straight over. She seems me coming and I can tell she's trying to decided which way would be the fastest to exit.

"Not so fast." I say grabbing her hand.

"Hey Michael." Avery says, Whinny looks anywhere but at me.

"Avery," I smile at her. "Whinny can I talk to you for a second?"

She hesitates "Oh sure." She says bye to Avery, gives her a hug and follows me to a corner of the cafeteria.

"You look nice today."

"Awe Michael, thanks" Okay, this is a good sign, she's opening up to me a little, I think.

"So the dance is this weekend."

"Yes, it is."

"Will you please make me happy and let me escort you?"

She gives me a look "I'm sorry, but I can't." She starts to walk off and I take her arm.

"Whinny, please stop ignoring me, I can't take it. I want and need you in my life. We still have nine months before anything is going to change. You're killing me. I am completely head over heels crazy about you!"

She looks away. "There's just, I really can't. It's complicated."

"Whinny what is going on?"

"Nothing." She says quickly.

"I'm not going to let anyone hurt you, I'm not going to hurt you. I don't know what you're so afraid of?" She looks at me and her eyes finally go soft "you promise?" It comes out almost as a whisper. I can tell she's somewhat scared, but also somewhat comforted by what I said.

"Of course not."

"But I don't want to hurt you." I pull her into a hug and she lets me, she wraps her arms around me and it's the best I've felt since the day she said goodbye. For being such an independent guy I honestly can't believe how much I depend on this girl. She means everything to me.

"I'd rather you hurt me and break me a million times, then never getting to see, talk to or touch you again. I'm a guy Whinny and I'm admitting that I want you in my life. I'm willing to take the risk." I've never had my heartbroken by a girl, but yes, for her I'd risk it.

She pulls back and studies me hard.

"Can you tell me why you flipped a switch so fast, it's like everything was perfect and then bam, you disappeared? I don't understand what could have changed as fast as it did."

I can tell she's thinking before responding with "I really think you just needed some space, and I think I did too. I don't just open up and trust and fall for people. I got scared."

"And I fell for you really fast too. I don't understand it, but that's the thing, when you find someone great I don't think you're supposed to understand it, or have it all make sense. I think you should just go with it. I was thinking and planning of the perfect and most romantic way possible to ask you out. Then you flipped." She smiles at me.

"I'm sorry, I just didn't want to be a rebound. And I wasn't ready to admit that I want you in my life."

I lean forward and kiss her forehead "you could never be a rebound, you're the first person I've ever met, to make me feel alive. You make me want to be a better person. And you've made me want to start living again." Which is very true. After Max I felt like I have just been going through the motions, until Whinny came into my life. I pull back and look at her. In this moment she seems so innocent, young, fragile and still somewhat scared. "Are you still unsure of wanting me in your life?"

"No."

"Okay with that being said and the air cleared, will you please go to the dance with me?"

"I'm so sorry, but I'm going with Jimmy."

"Whinny?"

"Look Michael Jimmy didn't want to go alone and we both know neither of us have feelings for each other so we're just going as friends. Maybe if you would have asked me sooner."

"How could I ask you when you've been ignoring me?"

"I…"

I cut her off, "I realize I'm late but I just assumed…"

"I was ignoring you to protect myself. I'm sorry if that doesn't seem fair, but I have a heart and feelings too. I realize I shouldn't have just ignored you and been a ghost, it just seemed easier that way. I thought maybe you'd forget about me and move on. I thought our lives would go back to before we met."

"Is that what you honestly want?"

"No." She smiles at me. "I've never once stopped thinking about you."

"Good."

She laughs and kisses me on the check. "Save me a dance?"

"Yeah" She puts her hands around me again and lays her head on my chest. "Michael, don't be mad. Everything's okay, it's all good."

"I'm not mad at you, I'm mad at myself." I take in her scent. "What is it about you that always makes me cave?" I wrap my arms around her. Actually I am a little mad at her, I mean damn it she walked out on our friendship and just assumed that I should have asked her sooner, when this whole time I haven't been able to find her. I guess I'll let it slide as long as I have her back.

She looks up at me with big green eyes "because I'm a very loveable person."

I smile, "that you are."

"As long as you promise you've got my back."

"How can I be sure you're serious, you broke the promise of not running away?"

She sighs "I can't tell you, but as long as you're in this with me, then I won't go anywhere again."

"I promise and I don't break those." She nods her head in agreement with me. "I just wish you'd tell me what's going on."

"I will Michael, when the time is right I will. But you can't leave." Her expression is serious. I wonder if this has anything to do with her black eye.

"I won't. I haven't given up this whole time and I sure as heck am not going to start now."

"Thank you." She whispers.

"Michael come on, we've got work to do." Kevin walks past with Lance, Shane and Joe. Whinny pulls back and lets me go.

"I'll see you later?" I ask and give her a look. "I know how you like to run away and disappear."

She looks sad, but laughs "I'm here, for good just like you told me that night at the football game, I'll always be here for you, near or far and yes, you will see me later." I walk away hating every step that takes me further from her.

I come downstairs in Khaki pants, a black button down all tucked in with a white tie, a black belt and black dress shoes. It's finally Friday, the night of the dance. I'm excited to have a weekend off football, well technically we still have practice tomorrow, but at least it's a short one. We actually start Sectional Tuesday. If we win, then we play Friday night and if we win that game then we'll play Saturday night for the championship.

"Oh Michael, you look so handsome." Mom snaps a photo.

"Mom can we please wait until Prom to do the whole picture thing?"

"I wish your date was here."

"Mom, we're going just as friends, and I promise I'll get a picture with her, just for you."

"Honey I'm going to follow you to her house."

"Mom, that's embarrassing"

"Just a few photos, Michael, it's your senior year." My date is actually Jamie, the junior who's the hostess at the Frying Pan. Whinny told me she wasn't going to go because she didn't have a date and all her friends did. So I asked her. She knows it's just as friends, but her face still lit up when I asked.

"Alright well let's go." I say grabbing my keys and heading outside. As I reach my truck Jimmy comes pulling up. He gets out and walks over to me.

"Hey Michael."

"What's up Jimmy?"

"Not much, hey thanks for not being upset about Whinny going to the dance with me."

"It's not easy." Just then Whinny comes out of her house in a strapless black dress that's tight on top and flares around the bottom. It stops above her knees showing off her very toned and athletic legs. She has a lime green bow tied around the mid-section, with half her hair pulled back with a matching bow. She looks simple yet so beautiful.

"Well don't you clean up real nice?" Jimmy walks up to her and gives her a kiss on the cheek. It makes me want to punch him.

"Thanks." She smiles at me.

"Breathtaking" is all I say. My mom comes out of our house and looks at Whinny with Jimmy.

"I knew you two would hook up sooner or later, especially with how much time you spend together, and him always running his hands all over you." She says rudely.

"Mom"

"Oh no Mrs. Statemen we aren't together. Neither of us had a date so we decided to go together, just as friends. But him running his hands all over me, has led us both to full ride scholarships. Thanks for noticing."

"Oh." I notice my mom's pretty much glaring at Whinny. That just pissed her off to the moon and back. I'm actually glad. Whinny nor Jimmy should have to take crap from anyone. What they do is pretty cool and it takes a lot of hard work and talent.

"Hey mom, you want pictures, take one of Whinny and me."

"Michael, you really need to get going." Mom's uncomfortable again.

"Just one." I walk up to Whinny and wrap my arm around her placing my hand on the small of her back and pulling her in close to me. She smells like strawberries. She stands facing me and puts one hand on my chest. I'm sure she can feel my heart speed up. Touching Whinny and being around her in general is just something my body craves. She brings me back to life. I feel like this past month I haven't really existed without her. Mom snaps the photo, it's hard for me to let go of her.

"Well time to go get Jamie, see you guys there."

"Bye."

Once Jamie and I finally escape mom's picture wrath we head to the dance.

"You look very pretty Jamie."

"Thank you." Jamie's short but athletic; she has thick blond hair that hangs past her shoulders, a cute round face and huge brown eyes. She looks like a puppy that you just can't help but adore.

"It's hard to believe your single. You have a great personality too. All those quick wit jokes you were pulling back there."

She laughs "Please, all you guys are alike for the most part, you don't care about a girl's personality. All you want are the hot, popular girls and vice versa, the girls just want to popular, hot guys. Who cares if their mean and treat you and others like crap, you're all just happy you get to be with her or him and go to social events. It's just all about popularity. I mean look at you and Jasmine."

"Ouch. Well first off I was popular without her, but I can see where you have a point. I use to think it was the greatest thing to be with the most popular girl, then one day I woke up and realized it doesn't mean anything to be with someone you don't have any feelings for. Status quo and statics aren't everything. And someday those other guys will all start thinking with the right head and realize that too."

"Yeah, when they finally find out their being cheated on, then they get really upset because they thought she or him was the love of their life, but really that's not why they're upset, they just cared about their popularity status."

"I feel like you might be speaking from experience?" She really is mad and upset. She looks like she's about to cry.

"I'm sorry, you're not like most guys that are popular." She sighs "I really like this one guy, and truth be told he likes me too, but he doesn't want to break up with his girlfriend because she makes him look good and puts him higher in our class rankings. It disgusts me. I know I'm not the cutest or most athletic, but I bring a lot to the table."

"So what? Are you just waiting on him to make his move?" She doesn't answer. "You need to make him jealous, make him realize what he's missing out on. Or you need to just move on. You're better than that Jamie. You aren't the type of girl to just sit around letting some guy toy with your feelings." She still doesn't say anything.

"I just don't understand high school."

"No one does." I say back. She sits there looking sad. "Is he going to be there tonight?"

She nods her head yes.

"I think you're in luck. After all you are going to the dance with the most eligible bachelor in the whole school."

"Yeah, but aren't you with Whinny?"

"Sort of, but you're also going to be around my friends, and many of them are single. And their all popular too, and we're seniors, so no matter what, you're going to be surrounded by good looking, single popular senior guys."

"You'd really help me?"

"Why not? We're already going together; let's make the most of it."

When we get to school I hold my arm out for Jamie. She hesitates but takes it.

"Tonight, follow my lead and you'll have this guy dying to be with you."

She laughs "okay." I can tell she's nervous. As we walk in I spot some of the guys right away. I'm eager to let Kevin in on the plan to make Jamie look good. I know he'll be excited to help.

"Tonight you're going to be surrounded by the senior football stars. The whole school loves us."

She laughs "I can handle that." As we approach the guys I notice Taz—the guy Jamie's into—watching us.

"Guys, this is Jamie, she's going to be our date this evening."

"Hi" she says

"This is Kevin, Joe and Shane."

"It's lovely to get to share you." Shane says. The Emcee starts talking about kicking this dance off right. The music gets turned up louder and we all make our way to the dance floor. Avery and Lance finally show up and join us. I see there's some tension though. And Parker and Lucy make their way over too. I notice Taz watching Jamie; I keep her next to me and Kevin. She's already laughing and twirling and just having fun. After a few songs I leave her with Kevin as I head to get a drink. Even he seems to be enjoying himself. It doesn't look as if he has anything on his mind. He's just enjoying the moment he's in.

Finally, a slow song comes on. I ask Jamie to dance. While everything's slow I finally find Whinny. She's talking to a few other girls. Jimmy's slow dancing with someone else and I even see Jasmine who's actually sitting this one out. The song ends and everything speeds up again. Kevin slides over and takes Jamie's hand. "My lady." I can tell she's already forgotten about Taz. She and Kevin seem to be hitting it off pretty good.

By the time the second slow dance comes around I leave Jamie and Kevin and seek out Whinny.

"Will you dance with me?"

"I'd love too." I pull her in close. "Thanks for bringing Jamie; she looks like she's having a great time."

"She's nice. I can see why you're fond of her."

Whinny smiles "she's a lot like me in a way." She rests her head on my chest.

"I can hear your heart beat."

"What's it saying?" She looks up at me with soft green eyes.

"That you're happy."

"For the first time since Max and dad, yes Whinny, I'm extremely happy. But I'd be even happier if I get to start calling you my girlfriend." I lean down towards her and we kiss. I can feel how much she needs me during this kiss and it's a feeling I can't describe. After the kiss she puts her head back on my chest. She laughs and I know it's because my heart beat has sped up. I laugh too "yeah, that's what you do to me."

"And yes Michael, but only if I get to call you my boyfriend." She winks at me.

After the song ends Whinny walks with me over to the guys and to say hi to Jamie, only Jamie isn't there. Lance and Avery decide to take off for the night.

"She doesn't like school functions does she?" Parker remarks

"She's weird, but cute."

"But weird."

"I haven't quite figured out how their personalities match up yet. Michael, seriously?"

"Well when you're one on one she's different I guess. So where's Jamie?"

"Oh she went to get a drink." I look over and sure enough Taz is over talking to her.

"He really doesn't deserve her."

"He's an ass; you should see him when he comes to the Frying Pan" Whinny puts in. "He comes in and flirts with her, honestly makes her believe she's the only one for him, then all of a sudden the girl he's with will walk in and he'll blow up on Jamie and tell her she's pathetic, and needs to find a different guy to stalk."

"I can't believe she puts up with that."

"Well is some sense I don't think she can let him go, because he won't let her go. He's written her love poems, sends her flowers. I've seen them make out. I think he keeps telling her he's going to end things with this other girl but never does. Then when Jamie's ready to tell him off, he pulls her back in again."

"Let me handle this." Kevin walks over and puts his arm around Jamie, says something to Taz and then he and Jamie start walking this way.

"Such drama." Kevin says acting like a girl, and we all somehow think it's funny and laugh.

"Whinny stay with me the rest of the night. I'm sure Jimmy won't mind; he seems pretty preoccupied." I wrap my arms around her tiny body from behind and place my head on her shoulder.

"I don't ever want to leave you." Her voice sounds soft. Those words make my knees go weak. I give her a little squeeze and we sway to the music even though it's a fast song. I know my decision to which college I will be attending is hard and I'm slightly scared that I'll choose the wrong school, but I realize I'm not the only one scared of what the future holds. All I know now is I'm scared I'm going to choose the school that takes me the furthest away from this girl.

A popular song comes on and I spin Whinny out. She laughs and starts dancing next to Jamie with me and Kevin behind the girls. The rest of the evening is very enjoyable. I actually had the most fun I've ever had at a school dance. Jasmine never got along well with the guys so I never got to stay with them for too long. It was always just me and her or me and her with her friends.

When the last song comes on Whinny announces that she has to go. I told her I could take her home but she insisted on letting Jimmy since she came here with him.

"You're not planning on running away are you?" I ask, I'll admit I'm still a little afraid she'll disappear on me again.

She takes my hand "no, we're in this, whatever this is, together." I lift her hand and kiss it.

"Alright, see you soon." She takes off towards the doors. In general, the night actually went pretty fast. It was nice to have a Friday night of something other than football. I think a slight refresher was in store for us guys and I'd say this just did the trick. The last song ends and Kevin and I escort Jamie outside, but Kevin actually offers to take her home, she agrees.

"Thanks for everything Michael." She hugs me then gets in Kevin's truck.

"No problem." I say closing the door. I smile at myself knowing things may end up working out differently, but overall we pulled the evening off and it was fun. Taz is definitely seeing Jamie in a new light, as is Kevin. I haven't seen him this into a girl in a long time. This time I think he may actually be pretty serious.

Chapter Twelve

When I get home I notice a silver car parked on the street in front our house. Mom must have some girls over.

"Michael." Whinny comes running up to me, still in her dress.

"Wow you did get home fast" All I really want to do is hold her in my arms and watch a movie.

"Listen to me; you need to go check on your mom."

"I'm sure she's fine, just a girl's night in probably."

"No Michael, please listen to me." I can tell she's scared and worried. "You said you had my back." It comes out barely audible.

"Okay." I walk around my truck with Whinny following. Just then a man comes out of the front door with mom pushing him off the porch.

"Please leave you aren't supposed to come here."

"Jane tell me why you've been ignoring me."

"You really have to leave!" my mom's voice is frantic "Michael will be home any minute."

"Already here" Mom finally looks in the direction of the driveway. She looks pale and like she might faint no surprise there though really.

"So what's going on?"

"Nothing, this man was just leaving."

"Jane."

"Hey." I look at the guy who is trying to step closer to her "back off my mother."

"Michael."

I am so confused right now. "Now mom, tell me what in the hell is going on." She points to Whinny who's behind me.

"This is your entire fault. You didn't listen to me and you told him. You ruined everything. I knew you would!"

"I didn't say a word; it wasn't my place too." Whinny says her voice small. That's who Whinny's been afraid of, MY mom? But why? I guess that would explain why mom hasn't been able to stand Whinny here lately.

"Don't you think if she would have told me anything I wouldn't be so damn confused? You'd think I'd know what's going on. But here I am, clueless so fill me in NOW!"

Mom starts crying "I'm so sorry sweetie."

Whinny comes up and wraps both her hands around my left arm. "Mrs. Statemen, you have to tell him. If you don't pull yourself together and tell him, then I will. I will finally let him know. He has to know."

"Michael." Mom says between breaths "your father and I are getting a divorce." I feel the air get knocked out of me. "And I'm pregnant with Rogers's baby." She points to the guy. Okay I lied, now all the air is knocked out of me. I've felt for weeks that I might actually have a breakdown, and now here it is. This is it. Whinny kisses the back of my arm through my shirt.

"It'll be okay." She whispers to me.

"Wait" I spin around jerking her hands away and face her. She steps back a little startled. "How did you know?"

It's like at one second everything comes back to me. Whinny's black eye, her ignoring me, mom hating Whinny ever sense the black eye, Whinny sayin' we were getting to close to fast and disappearing for a second time and mom just in general being gone and spacey. Mom being happy that Whinny wasn't around me anymore. The person who's been in control of Whinny has been my mom. And every time she started to get close mom did something, I don't know what but she pushed us apart. The best thing to ever to happen to me and she pulled us apart.

Whinny doesn't answer me.

"Whinny please, not you too, don't do this."

"Frying Pan does carryout. I delivered to her office and happened to overhear their conversation about the baby. They saw me and stopped me before I could leave." I look back at my mom, crying on the porch and this guy standing in the yard.

"How did you get that black eye?"

"Michael."

"How Whinny?" I'm too upset to think.

"They were afraid I was going to tell you. So they made sure I didn't, and they've had tabs on me this whole time. That's why I backed out of the picture, I was I guess getting to close. And I WANTED to tell you. Every time you asked me I told you I couldn't talk about it, but I wanted to. And I WANTED to be with you. This whole time I've WANTED you and it killed me to stay away. I still WANT you." And with that, I take off and tackle the man who destroyed my family, the little family I had left. I punch him and he punches back causing me to roll off. We both get up at the same time.

"Stop it!" Mom yells. I throw another punch "Michael!" I throw another punch and another, I can't stop myself, all the rage that's been building up ever since Max's death and dad leaving and now this. I hear crying in the background and screaming but then. Then I hear Whinny.

"Michael, please." I look over at her. I can't explain what happened, but she's standing there looking at me, with a look of needing me. She needs me to be the bigger person. She looks tiny and afraid and I just break inside. I look back at this guy who's now kneeling on the ground with a bloody face. I grab his shirt by the collar and pull him up.

"You're not worth it." Then I throw him to the ground. I look at mom who's standing there crying. I spit out some blood and walk over to Whinny. We stand facing each other; I let out a deep breath.

"Whinny." I need her too. She pulls me in and I lay my head on her shoulder and wrap my arms around her. She strokes the back of my hair.

"I know it hurts. I'm so sorry. I wanted to tell you." I feel a tear drop fall from her face and land on my check.

"You kept this from me." I pull back and look at her. I can tell it's really been bothering her. I hold my hand out and she takes it, we head to my truck. I open the door and she climbs in while moms over helping that dumbass.

"Michael don't go! I'm sorry!" she yells. I close the door and drive. I end up driving down to the beach, neither of us saying anything. Whinny gets out and follows me down the beach in silence until I just stop and sit down in the sand. She sits down next to me and puts one tiny hand on my knee. We continue to sit in silence listening to the sound of the waves roll in. And I cry, silently. A year ago my life was nothing like this. How can a year change so many things?

"Whinny?"

"Yes."

"You knew this whole time and didn't tell me? I'm hurt."

She sighs. "I'm sorry. It hurt me every day, it killed me Michael, I wanted to, but it wasn't my place. And to be honest I don't think you would have believed me. So that was the reason why I backed away. I didn't want to hurt you."

We're silent for a minute or two before I say "I got even for you."

"Just like you said you would." She kisses my check. "A man who sticks to his word. I like that." I wipe away blood still coming from my lip.

"Whinny what did you mean when you said they had 'tabs on you'"

"Believe it or not, they were watching you, and me, very closely. They knew the day you drove me to the humane society, they knew I was going to school more because they would come into the Frying Pan and ask for me and I wouldn't be there and they had my phone number from when I made the delivery to their office. Your mom was always out late because she was watching to make sure I wouldn't get close to you. They both were. They didn't want me near you until they told you the news, but the kept refusing until they had things figured out themselves."

"Can I trust you?" I ask

"Well I didn't tell your mom's secret now did I. And I happen to like you more than I do your mom." After some silence she says "I know this is hard to digest and understand."

"I don't think you do. I mean no offense but I lost my brother, it hasn't even been a year yet, it still hasn't sunk in. Then my dad leaves because of it, which causes my mom to leave him and then on top of it, she's having another guy's baby." Whinny falls back into the sand and lays there a minute, then sits back up.

"Yeah, it's a lot to take in. And it's not fair that it's all falling on you. Sometimes life is pretty crappy like that, but you've got to just keep going and eventually it will all work itself out."

She's being real and honest with me, she's not sweet coating anything and even though it hurts to hear, I like it. I need the truth, and honesty and reality.

"You always being positive is making it hard to feel sorry for myself right now." I say sarcastically.

She laughs "it's not easy to always be positive and there are times when I'm not."

"I want to tell you something." She says after a couple minutes of more silence. "I'm going to tell you the deepest secret of my life. Only one other person knows and that's Avery." I look at her in the moonlight. This is it, I'm finally going to know the secret she's so scared of. Beside my mom. "Michael, I don't have any parent's."

"What?"

"The people I live with, well they're my grandparents and they basically hate me." I don't say anything so she continues. "Their son—which is my dad—got a girl knocked up at age sixteen. They wanted her to 'fix or take care of' the problem. My dad and my mother then decided to run away together. But what were they going to do; they had no money and were high school drop outs. Anyways after I was born my mother was having complications and passed away two day later. My dad tried to find her parents a couple weeks after but he couldn't. They were no longer here. So he did the next best thing, left me in a basket with a note on his parent's doorstep. My dad then proceeded to commit suicide. He knew he couldn't raise me on his own, especially at that age, and I guess he wasn't sure his parents would forgive him. I guess he thought death was a better option. I like to think that he loved my mom so much that he wanted to go be with her. But his last wish was that I had a roof over my head and food on the table until I'm an adult. Because they loved him, they kept me to see his final wish through. But they hate me, because I caused their only child to take his own life, and trust me, they don't let me forget." My jaw actually drops open.

"That day I came out of the house and you and Avery were standing there. We had gotten in a fight, they had taken that kitten from me, even though I kept it in my room and it never made a sound. They wouldn't stand for having any other 'filthy living animal' in the house. And they just kept repeating, 'you're so ungrateful, you're such a spoiled brat, you're the reason your dad left, he couldn't stand the thought of raising you.' And after so long, yeah those words do get to you." She starts to cry. She takes a minute then continues.

"They don't take business trips. They're retired and have time shares. Sometimes they leave for a whole month. I work because I pay some of the bills because I'm in their words 'the one living there and using everything.' Also partly why the house is always dark. Ha but they give me two hundred dollars a month and I am to make do with that. Now don't get me wrong they'll pay the bills when they're here, and they pay for my schooling, but that's it. If I want something, I have to pay for it myself, like my clothes. Which is also why I walk everywhere. I can't afford a vehicle, let alone insurance on it. Some months I'm little more strapped for cash than others. Like the months that they happen to be gone when all the bills are due at the same time. Thankfully that's only happened twice. I miss a lot of school so I can work. I've also been saving for college. Avery has really helped me out a lot this year. She brings me the homework I've missed and turns it in for me too."

"That's why you're like the wind."

"What?"

"Nothing, go on."

"Listen Michael, I'm not telling you this to make you feel sorry for me, or to minimize what just happened in your life. I'm telling you this because I trust you and I know you'll keep my secret safe. I'm just letting you know bad things can happen to good people."

"How can they not love you? You're their grandchild, their only grandchild that they'll ever have."

"That was born out of wedlock. I ruined their perfect son's life." She takes a breath. "Stunting with Jimmy isn't easy. Yes, it hurts and I've fallen way more than I'd like to admit, but I need this. It's my only way out. Once we signed for our scholarships I started coming to school more because I know part my college will be paid for, but yet there has to be so many days of attendance."

I know in the dark she's looking at me, but for some reason I can't bring myself to look at her. Here I am feeling sorry for myself thinking about my life falling apart, but poor Whinny has never had hers together.

"I'm very proud of the person I've become, I've worked hard for everything I have or have been given and honestly I'm so grateful. I know you can't see the light right now Michael and you don't have too. But give it time. Everything will be okay. Eventually time does heal everything." Whinny scoots forward, turns her back to me and falls into my chest. I pull my knees up and wrap my arms around her.

She talks again. "You have a lot going for you. Don't let this ruin what you yourself have worked so hard for. Your mother wasn't the one out there putting in countless hours in the rain, snow, and heat. She wasn't the one experiencing excruciating practices."

No instead she was out there putting it out there for someone else. But even so as I sit holding her I just can't believe the things she's told me. I can't believe her life has never consisted of a real true family feel. I may be missing over half of mine but at least for a while I HAD one and I have precious memories from that. I really can't fathom everything she's just told me. No parents? That's how I feel right now, but I've never experienced life without them.

"Whinny, how did you turn out so great and not hating everything and the world?"

"Well when I was younger I had you and your brother. You guys always made me feel better about life. I loved your family, y'all somehow made me feel like I was a part of something real. When you and Max stopped playing with me I went through some dark days. Grandma and grandpa were always unhappy about something and blaming it on me. So I looked for something that would keep me out of the house for as long as possible. I got into cheerleading and it saved me." She tips her head back and looks at me. "So in a way, I guess I'm glad you stopped having anything to do with me, but I'm also glad you're back. I've never hated anything, because your mom used to talk about how much else was out there in life. And believe it or not, love concurs hate. And I love cheerleading. All we had to do is want something bad enough. For instance, you with football. Don't get me wrong I thought about running away, but then I wouldn't have a place to stay, or an education, or any money or any food. And I knew I could put myself in a dangerous situation being a young girl and out on my own. My grandparents are mean and love to yell at me and blame things on me, but they never physically abuse me. I can handle most of their verbal abuse, I just learned to tune it out."

"You really are one of a kind. Since the day you came over and watched that movie with me—back in August, two months ago—I've regretted not getting to spend the last ten years with you." She scoots up and turns then lays her head in my neck.

"What did I say about regrets? I strongly dislike that word. The past is the past Michael. But your mom is right, there's bigger and better things outside of Southport, don't give up on that." We don't say anything else. We sit like this until I can't keep Whinny from shivering anymore then we head back to my truck.

"Why won't you tell me where you're going to school?" I ask once we're inside and I have the heat turned on.

"I don't want my decision to affect yours. I know you're being offered a lot of scholarships and to good schools. I don't want you to choose a school just because I did."

"Do you really think I'd do that?"

"A little bit."

"Why?"

"I think you'd know that better than me." She smiles, "But also because for the first time in a long time you have real feelings. I see the way you look at me; I feel the way you touch me. I want you to know those feelings are mutual. I'm just afraid you'll think too much about it. You need to choose the school that feels the best for you. Whatever happens between us will happen but no matter what you'll never lose me as a friend again. It killed me to not talk to you. But I was scared of what your mom and Roger would do to me, or even to you." She really is good at this reading people stuff. I think I need to pick out someone I know, like Kevin and have Whinny read him just to prove to me that it's not just me she can read.

"Just follow your heart when picking your school." She says.

"Whinny" I turn in my seat and look at her "when I look at you, I see the most amazing young woman I've ever met and you make me want to be a better person. I want you to think I'm the greatest guy ever. I want you to be proud of me."

"Michael."

"Everything has been better in my life when you're around. You make things seem easy, even when I know they're not, like tonight for instance."

"I am proud of you." She slides over next to me and takes my hand. "I'm proud of the way you stood up to Jasmine and told her she needs an attitude adjustment if she wanted to stay with you. I'm proud of you for working so hard at football, because deep down you know a scholarship is your only way out of this town too. I'm proud of how you stepped up to the plate and how you handled the news about your brother, about your dad leaving. And I'm proud that through all of this you're still carrying a 3.9 g.p.a.," she smiles.

"You would throw school into this."

"Just trying to lighten the mood. But most of all Michael, I'm proud of you standing up for not only myself, but your mom too. She made a mistake, a huge mistake, but we're all human and we all make mistakes. My mistake was walking away from you. I knew you needed me and I knew I need you, I shouldn't have just walked out on that. But love runs deeper than judging a person by one thing they did wrong. And I'll be the most proud of you when you walk through the door to your house and you forgive her. It doesn't' have to be now, or even in six months. Maybe not even a year from now, but forgiveness is key." I lean my head against the window.

"That's easier said than done."

"I know."

"Whinny, I know in seven months we'll be graduating and possibly moving in separate directions, but thank you for taking this leap with me."

"Nothing would make me happier." I lean forward taking both hands, wrapping them around her neck and we kiss.

"Come here." I say after the kiss. I wrap my arms around her. This is the only place I want to be.

"So how many schools offered you scholarships?" I ask trying to get my mind off EVERYTHING else that was just said.

"Three Big Ten schools, four SEC schools and then five small decent colleges."

"You don't want to give any hints away?"

"Well…."

"Alright how about you give me at least two that you didn't choose."

"Ole Miss, and Vanderbilt."

"I'm guessing you went Big Ten then?"

"I'm guessing you'll just have to wait and see." I smile and kiss the top of her head. Even though tonight's been pretty shitty, this conversation with Whinny has kept me on cloud nine.

"Let's get you home." She says a little while later.

"I don't want to go home."

"Michael, it's okay. It's just to sleep. I'll come save you tomorrow." Because I'm tired I give in. We drive, Whinny keeps my mind off things by talking about the dance. She noticed how jealous Taz was that Jamie wouldn't even look at him and she thought it was ironic that Jamie went home with Kevin but she could see a possibility for the two. It seemed refreshing to talk about something so easy and light hearted compared to everything that was just said on the beach. But I'm not quite here all the way. When I get back home I notice the silver cars still here.

"Hey Whinny." I reach for my gym bag thrown in back. "Will you do the honor of wearing my football jersey on Tuesday?" I hand her my away jersey.

"I'd love too." She takes it then looks at my house which for two in the morning still has all the lights on. "Do you want me to go in with you?"

"No, I think you've seen enough for one night." We get out and stand in front of my truck. "You really do mean a lot to me." I say pulling her close. I kiss her forehead.

"You mean a lot to me too Michael." She slowly slips out of my grasp and I watch her unlock her house and head inside. I wish I could take away the verbal abuse Whinny has had to suffer. I really don't understand why her grandparents won't love her. Her dad made a mistake, but they shouldn't take it out on her.

Finally, I turn for my home. Inside the guy is laying on the couch with ice on his face and mom's pacing between the living room and kitchen.

"Dear Lord Michael. You need ice."

"I don't want anything. I want to go to bed."

"Honey, I think we need to talk about this." Mom tries to approach me but I back up.

"NOW you want to talk? Seriously mom I've been asking you for the past month to talk to me."

"Michael, I didn't know how to tell you. I freaked and panicked every time you asked me questions." She stops trying to think what she wants to say.

"You haven't come to a single football game all year. Tell me why. Was it because you were spending all your time with this guy? Trying to decide what to do about the baby? Here I thought you were working overtime to make money for me to go to school. I think very little of you right now mom. I am truly disappointed. I'm still here, I didn't walk out on you when Max died, I didn't walk out on you when dad decided to re-enlist and go overseas. I stayed and I became the man of the house all for you and this is how you treat me?" She starts crying again, silently this time.

"And worst of all when I'm going through this terrible journey, you tried keeping the one person away from me who I needed and wanted in my life the most!" I look at her. "I'm going to bed." I start up the stairs and slam my bedroom door shut. I officially know where I want to go to college. It won't be easy to sign the papers not knowing where Whinny is going, but for myself this is what I have to do.

Chapter Thirteen

It's Tuesday. I can't believe what I'm feeling, which is nothing. I'm been trying to focus on tonight but I just can't. I haven't talked to mom at all since Saturday night. She keeps trying but I've been ignoring her. I even spent all day at the Frying Pan on Sunday to finish homework and because I couldn't handle being at home with her. Whinny and Jamie both kept me occupied throughout the day too. They'd each come over and talk to me and then I even helped bus tables. It was way better than being at home.

Jamie was still on cloud nine from the dance and how much she really likes Kevin. She can't believe how fast her opinion of Taz has changed. She said he tried calling her Sunday and she refused to answer. It's nice to see her happy, she deserves it.

Mom tried explaining to me that she and Dad agreed that the divorce is mutual and that dad knows she's seeing another guy. They just haven't been happy for a while and then with Max's death it was just time for them to go their separate ways. I've brushed those facts off. How can you be married to someone for 28 years and just let the other person go? It's not that I hate my mom. I'm just really disappointed in the way she handled everything and to throw all of this at me right before Sectionals. I know she didn't mean too, but it's hard to concentrate on anything else.

I realize I'm just standing in front of my locker, starring at my books but nothing's happening. I need to close the door and get to lunch; I'm sure seeing all the guys will help brighten my spirits. None of them know. I want to tell Kevin, but I can't. This is my problem not theirs and I don't want to risk putting the other guys in a mood. The whole school is pumped for tonight, well everyone in the whole school, except for the quarterback. They've made banners and signs and the cheerleaders even decorated our lockers. Whinny decorated mine with our school colors, my name across the top and a big— almost like a fathead—picture of myself in action.

"Michael." Next thing I know Whinny is standing next to me, and just like I asked she's wearing my away football jersey and her cheerleading sweat pants. She pulls me back and closes the locker door. "The whole school is talking about your eye. You know it's kind of sexy." From getting into the punching match with mom's new lover, I came out with a huge black and blue eye and a busted lip. Everyone has been wondering and asking how I got it.

I don't say anything to Whinny or move.

"Look at me." She says and I finally look into her green eyes. In her eyes I see the truth and right now I just can't handle the truth. "Tonight isn't just about you. Tonight is about you and your team. All those guys that have put in countless hours of practicing, they need this more than you do. There's a good chance half of them won't move on to college and get to play. Don't let this be their last game. Don't let them down Michael. If there's one thing I know you don't like to do, it's letting people down."

I give her a small smile "My saving grace."

"Tonight's about having fun and enjoying one of the last times you'll get to play with this group of guys; and I think we should start celebrating now." She throws my left arm over her shoulder and wraps her arm around my waist and starts guiding me towards the cafeteria. I stand up a little taller, more than happy to have her by my side. Having Whinny on my side has honestly been the best thing that's happened to me since my brother's death. She somehow knows all the right things to say at any given moment. And now that we are officially official, we've been pretty much inseparable even if it's only been four days. As we grab our treys and head to the table with the guys, Jasmine approaches and stops us.

"Michael, how's your eye? I can't believe how hanging out with her has turned you into such a bad person." She looks at Whinny. "You know; I've worn that jersey for the last three years."

"And I'm wearing it when it really counts, ya know, the LAST time, but no hard feelings."

"And for the record, me getting into a fight has nothing to do with Whinny." I throw in.

"Ha, well anyways good luck tonight Michael; I'm sure you'll do great like always." She starts in for a kiss on the check when I back away. She looks at me in surprise.

"It's a kiss on the check, I'm not poisonous."

"I'm dating Whinny and I don't CHEAT. You of all people should know that." I put a huge emphasis on cheat.

"Well you also said you didn't want a girlfriend."

"And I believe you're the one who said, some people like having or being in a relationship. You're right, I've found a great girl and I like being with her." Jasmine narrows her eyes at us. Whinny and I step pass and head to the table with the guys. Whinny and I have agreed to sit with each other at lunch for most of the days and at least the days she comes to school. Some days it'll be with her friends, which are basically the cheerleaders, and others it'll be with the guys.

"Hey Michael, hey Whinny." Kevin greats us and sitting by him is Jamie. She's actually wearing his away jersey. When giving a girl your jersey to wear it signifies that she's taken and she's supporting you, all around it's a good feeling and usually a pretty big deal. Most guys even if they're dating someone, won't let them wear one of their jerseys because like I said, that means you're actually taken.

"I kind of like having girls at the table." Kevin says looking at Jamie.

"Me too, as long as they can't respect us talking about guy stuff." Joe says.

"As long as you aren't talking about whose fart smells worse, I think we can handle it." Avery answers walking up with Lance and sitting on the other side of Whinny. Everyone laughs, we're not that disgusting.

"Hey girl."

"Hey, looking good."

"I'm glad you decided to join us." Parker and Lucy even come over and sit down.

"Awe, I feel like we're one big happy family." Shane smiles then taps Joe on the shoulder "Looks like we're going to have to find us some gal palls."

"Oh Shane, what did Keeley want? Did you ever call her back?"

"Yeah I did. And nothing, she actually called to apologize. She said she's finally going to a psychiatrist and she's on meds and feeling stable. But her doctor told her in order to feel better she needed to clean up her past. So she was calling everyone she'd ever hurt or gotten into a fight with and was just clearing the air. It was nice to talk her like a normal person."

"Good." The causal banter continues throughout lunch talking about the dance and what we all found intriguing about the night. We talked about some movies that are coming out, homework and started telling funny animal stories. None of us seem to want to talk about the game. I think it's because we're all excited, but really we're all just as nervous. I see Kevin, watching me, he can tell something's wrong but he doesn't say anything. I really haven't said much the past two days.

Whinny puts her hand on my knee and keeps it there most of lunch. When I look at her she smiles, I put my hand on top of hers. Her touch really calms me. Sadly, though I'm in this fucked up funk and she seems to be the only thing keeping me from losing it. I've got to shake this before the game, after all it's not like she can stand next to me during it.

After lunch the cheerleaders put on a pep rally for us and tonight. I watch Whinny and Jimmy doing they're stunting. I smile still in shock that she's my girl. Then Jasmine starts introducing the players for tonight, one by one each of us heads up when they call our names.

"Now, let's give it up for our quarterback! Michael Statemen!" The gym erupts in applause and noise. Now, finally now I'm starting to feel hyped and ready for tonight. Seeing Whinny up in the air with my jersey on and everyone knowing she's supporting me kind of helps too.

It's game time. I'm pacing back and forth in the locker room. All the other guys and coaches have headed out to the field. I want this win, I really do. I know when I step on the field nothing else will matter, there will be nothing else on my mind. I can do this. When I come onto the field I see the fans of both teams going wild. Welcome to Sectionals.

First play we run I get sacked, second play I get sacked again, third play the pass is incomplete and defense comes out. Slow rocky start. I only get my team halfway down the field and then we punt. We're down 14-0 with 3 minutes left in the second quarter. I know I shouldn't do it, but while the defense is in I glance up to the bleachers. Mom's here for the first time all year, and standing next to her is that guy. I rip my helmet off and vomit in the trash can. Half the audience see's and goes "Oooohhhh." I mean it's never a good sign when your quarterback is sick. I sit back down on the bench. Focus, come on this is everything. And Whinny's right it's not just for me, it's for all these guys sitting and standing here with me. We've come this far as a team; we can't just give up because of one bad apple. I watch as the other team runs right past our tackles. Thankfully he steps out of bounds at the 15-yard line.

"Dude, what the hell is going on?" Kevin sits down by me.

"I can't talk about it. Game time let's go."

"I love you like a brother man but we've got to get our asses in gear. Have you looked at the scoreboard?"

"Michael." I turn and all of a sudden Whinny's kneeling in front of me. "I've got this Kevin; can you give us minute." He gives her a look then gets up. "I'm not allowed to be over here so listen up." She grabs the front of my jersey and pulls me close, her eyes dart back and forth furiously.

"I need you. I need you to be my hero, I need you to come save me from the tower with the evil dragon, and that evil dragon is this other team. You have to defeat them to save me. So Michael will you let go of everything else? Will you please just enjoy this moment and will you come save me? You'll never be able to get to me if you don't destroy this dragon. Do you want to protect me? I need you too. And I need it now. I need you to play Michael, I need you to play like you've never played before." With that she gets up and quickly heads back to the cheerleading section.

Holy hell. She's good. I look up and glance at the scoreboard. And with that it's like I become a whole new guy. She needs me and she wants me to do this for her and because I know in my heart I love her I will. I put my helmet back on and watch as we stop them on a third down. They punt and we're able to get it to the forty-yard line. Our offense runs out to the field.

I jump up and down it's like all the feeling in my body has finally come back, I'm not a walking zombie anymore. "Alright offense, let's move this ball like we've done all freaking year. Wide rush outside on Bell."

"Bell?"

"Bell."

"Michael we haven't been playing the best, I don't think we should attempt that now. Let's just get the ball down the field."

"That's exactly what we're going to do on BELL!" We all break to line up. I'm feeling wide awake and ready to take on this team!

"Hut Hut Hike!" Screens are set and I take off running, I throw the lateral back to Shane, he's got blockers in front of him including me, he keeps moving past me. I get set and he throws another lateral back to me. I take my stance and aim downfield where Kevin cuts across wide open. I throw, he catches and he runs the last ten yards in for a touchdown.

"Hell yeah! Let's win us a ball game!" The crowd goes wild as Tucker, our kicker, comes into the game. The extra point is good. We go into half time only down by one touchdown.

"Alright boys, looks like we're waking up a little here. Now that play looked really good. I bet they aren't going to be expecting a lot more like it. So we're going to run everything we've got at them, even the plays that we ran in practice that weren't so great. Tonight we're going big, or else we're going home. And I sure as hell don't' think y'all want to go home."

When we come out of the locker room I look over at Whinny, wearing my jersey over the top of her cheerleading uniform. She's high in the air, but instead of cheering with the other members she's looking directly at me giving me the "give them hell look" I smile to myself. She's right; everything is going to be okay. I don't really know when, but if I just take one day, one second at a time I know I'll be alright. I'm back, I'm me again. I'm doing what I love most and I have the girl I love the most with me, supporting me.

"Hey." Kevin slaps me on the back as we approach the bench "I really love that girl. I don't know what she said to you but damn! You doing okay?"

"I'm back and I'm ready to kick this cougar's team's ass!"

"That's my boy!"

We didn't exactly kick their ass. We're all standing at the out of bounds line. It's like slow motion. They just scored a touchdown, with no time remaining in this game. They get one chance to make this field goal; if they do we'll be tied 21 all, which would mean overtime. I'm holding my breath and saying a prayer at the same time.

The balls hiked, the kicker approaches, the balls up and flying through the air. It's so quiet you can hear a pin drop. And he misses. He misses just by the hair on his chin, it angles left. He missed slightly to the left. It's like someone turns off the freeze fame. Us players all jump and start celebrating. The crowd goes wild. It was a hell of a good game and we advance and that's all that matters. The other team's kicker falls to the ground and his players pick him up, it isn't up to just one person to win a game, but it does help when all your players show up to play.

Chapter Fourteen

Friday at school Whinny is wearing my home jersey this time, and I'm wearing the away. She's over talking to Jimmy about a new stunt they're supposed to be doing tomorrow night. I'm at my locker leaning against it waiting for her so we can walk together to lunch. Whinny's pretty much my everything and I know that sounds lame for me to say since I'm a guy and all, but she's my kryptonite. She's what helped our team advance, she got my head back in the game. I'm still having a hard time wrapping my mind around her home life situation, but she doesn't ever seem to want to talk about it, so we don't. I'm also still having a hard time wrapping my mind around my current home situation, but I don't want to talk about it, so I don't.

I see Jasmine walking this way wearing Trey Jenkins jersey. He's a junior on the defense side, I don't really know him all that well.

"Looking good stud." She says stopping next to me.

"I see you found a jersey to wear, looks like you're a cool kid again."

"Funny, you should be a comedian." Then she says "I miss you."

"I think you just miss all the attention you got from being with me during times like this." She doesn't say anything. Maybe she really has changed a little. Usually she'd make a comeback by now. I look over at Whinny still talking with Jimmy.

"You really like her don't you?"

"I really really do."

"As much as it kills me to say this, I'm happy for you." I look at Jas, I can tell she's being sincere.

"Thanks."

"You think it'll work when you decide to go to separate colleges?"

"How do you know we'll go to separate colleges?"

"Please, Michael, you're too good not to play and she's too good not to cheer. What are the odds you two end up at the same school?"

"I don't know, but that's actually not what I'm thinking or worried about at the moment."

"I heard she already signed to cheer, do you know where?"

"I don't, do you?"

"No. But she and Jimmy deserve it." I want so desperately to know where Whinny's going to college. I asked Jimmy once but apparently Whinny's asked him not to tell anyone. And he said he was okay with that. I don't think he's too entirely happy with the decision but let's face it he wouldn't have a scholarship if it weren't for Whinny stunting with him. Finally, Whinny comes over towards Jasmine and I.

"Sorry that took longer than I was anticipating." I stand up tall and put my arm around her. I know Jasmine hates seeing me this affectionate with Whinny but I seriously can't help it.

"I guess I'll see you guys tomorrow. Fly away skirts Whinny."

"Alright, thanks." After Jasmine walks off Whinny leans up and gives me a kiss on the check. "I've wanted to do that for a while now." I smile. She lays her head against my chest. "I can hear your heart beat."

"What's it saying?"

"That you're nervous for tomorrow and excited."

"That sounds pretty spot on." She pulls back and takes my hand, "come on let's go get lunch, we're missing out on all the good table talk! Plus, I'm starved."

"Ha, good table talk." Whinny actually likes sitting at the table with all the guys, but it's helped too that Jamie sits with us and usually Lance and Avery will too. Lucy sometimes sits with Parker but she likes to be with her friends too. When we walk through the doors to the cafeteria the lunch room starts clapping and cheering and whooping and hollering. Yeah everyone's definitely excited about tomorrow. As we walk towards the line everyone stops to either say something to Whinny or to me. I never knew she was so popular but apparently she's everyone's favorite cheerleader. Must be all the wicked stunts. It helps that she's been at school more here too lately. Ever since she found out she was getting a full ride she hasn't been as worried about working as much.

"I think tomorrow will be pretty awesome." I say to her. She squeezes my hand.

"Of course it will. It's football Sectionals!"

After school Whinny comes running up to me before I even have a chance to finish putting all my books away.

"I'm so very happy to see you too." I say

"I wanted to make sure I caught you before you left. I have something I want to show you, but we have to travel to get there and I know we don't have much time."

I'm intrigued. "Where too?" She takes my hand.

"Just come on!" I lace my fingers with hers and we take off practically running for the parking lot. I do exactly as I'm told and 10 minutes later we end up parked at the cemetery my brothers in.

"Follow me." She gets out.

"Whinny, I can't." I say. I know she wants me to see Max, but I can't deal with all this before a game. I already still have enough things I'm trying to forget in order to get through this.

"Please, Michael, do this for me." She holds her hand out to me. Damn it. I reach out for it and we walk to his grave. Sitting there on his grave is a white envelope and some flowers.

"I actually come visit your brother a lot. I'm sure this isn't where you feel the closest to him but I wanted you to see this." She points at the envelope. "I also wanted him to read it."

I slowly pick it up. "So the flowers are from you?"

"Yes, I've brought many things out here. He died fighting for our country, for our freedom, it's the least I can do." I bow my head in a moment of silence. I've never thought about it that way before. I never come out here because she's right, this isn't where I feel closest to him, but he is a fallen solider and to that respect should be given.

"Are you sure you want me to read this?" She nods her head.

I open the envelope which reads:

Max and Michael, I hate you both, I hate you because even though you were

Mean to me, I still like you guys. I still think you're the good guys out there.

And those are hard to find. I'm sure my dad was a good guy, but I guess I'll

Never really know. I'm writing this to you both to let you know you've been

An inspiration to me. As in don't give up, no matter what life throws at me.

I've seen courage out of both of you, and maturity long beyond our age. I've

Seen laughter and I've seen love. You let me know there's something great

I just have to work hard to find it. Which is why I'm pushing so much with

Cheerleading. I want to pursue my dreams. Thank you for letting me be there

The whole time, even if I was invisible. Because you both taught me many

Things. I know in a few years we'll all move on and out of this town. I know

You'll forget me, but I won't ever forget you two. Thanks for keeping me here

In this town and safe for a little longer, thank you for making me want to

Continue to get my degree, and thank you for setting me free. I'm going to go

Out there and chase my dreams. I hope you both do too and let nothing stand

In your way.

Whinny.

I glance at the date. It was written our freshman year.

"I don't understand."

"That was when I was about to run away, I was so mad, and I had so much anger I didn't know what to do. I came home and you and your brother were outside playing football in the front yard, your mom and dad were on the porch and I was about to break when I saw all that."

I look at her, hurt that she wrote to us, but yet somewhat inspired. Even though we had nothing to do with Whinny she still found the good in us, to help make her a better person.

"So I went in and was going to write about how much I hated everything and was going to run. But once I started writing I had nothing bad to say, my pen only would write nice things and as I was going, I came across perspective. So I never ran. I obviously never sent this and actually I had forgotten all about it. I was cleaning out my closest the other day to find some stuff to sell and I found it. I thought now, with everything going on in your life, you could use some perspective yourself. And a little pick me up. You showed me to never give up, fight for what you want, I'm hoping now I can show that to you." I pull her in and kiss her forehead. Even when she didn't know me, she still figured out a way to help the future me.

"Thank you."

She smiles and I can see sparkle in her eyes.

"Come on, we've got a game to win."

And we did just that.

I can't keep still. It's now Saturday. Our final game is tonight. It's two o clock now and the games at eight. Mom's sitting at the kitchen counter reading a magazine and watching me pace through the house. We still haven't really talked about what happened. All I know is the guy or Roger hasn't been around me since. His bruises have supposedly healed and so have mine, well other than the ones I have from the football games.

"I can't believe you let him hit a girl. Don't you think he'll treat you the same way?" I finally let out a deep breath. Mom looks up. It really has been bugging me that he caused Whinny to have a black eye.

"It was an accident Michael. He never meant to hit her. She was setting the food down on the table and he was flinging his arms, all excited and scared and confused about the news I had told him. He was talking with his hands and arms and accidently elbowed her.

We both felt terrible about it. And we apologized" I start pacing the living room again. "I never meant to be rude to Whinny; I'm actually very fond of her. But I knew with you two having a growing friendship that she might have told you. So I told her to stay away from you. She very easily obliged when you started dating Avery. It wasn't easy though when you two broke up."

"Yeah you kept the best thing that's ever happened to me, away from me. When she would ignore me I felt like I was in a dark whole, she was the only thing keeping me floating and you were trying to keep that away. Do you even realize how hard this past month has been without her being around? Oh wait, no you wouldn't because you haven't been around either!"

Mom looks pale and hurt. "Michael I didn't realize, I'm sorry."

"I don't want to talk about it anymore. I shouldn't have even brought it up."

"You're right, let's talk about the game tonight. Don't be nervous sweetie, you guys blew that team out of the water last night and you're going to do the same tonight."

"I'm confident we will win as long as I don't look at you and Roger." I know it's a mean thing to say, but he's not my dad and he never will be. After Tuesday and what a mess I was after looking at them two together I knew I couldn't look into the stands anymore. Anytime I felt an uneasy feeling come over me, I looked at Whinny and it would pull my mind back to the game.

"I really am so sorry Michael. I know this wasn't fair to you. Especially not after everything else that has happened."

"Yeah, yeah, I said let's not talk about it." Mom and I would go through and have small snippets of this conversation at times. She was filling in some of the gaps for me, but right now really isn't a good time to talk about it. I'm supposed to meet some of the guys at five to go over a few things and of course just to hang out and talk smack about the other team. We all are very much ready to get this next game over with.

I get a text message and practically dive on my phone that's sitting on the couch.

"Michael you need to calm down, save this energy for tonight."

"Whinny's here!" I rush to the front door and open it. Standing on the porch is Whinny dressed in her cheerleading uniform sweats with my away jersey over the top. Her hairs pulled back in a long ponytail and she's got my number painted on her face.

"It's so good to see you!" I wrap my arms around her, lift her up and spin her around on the front porch. She smells like strawberries. When I set her down she giggles and kisses my ear.

"I wanted to come see you before tonight's game. I actually have to head to the Frying Pan though I'm working from three to seven."

"Come on in. Are you working in that?"

"I am; I want the whole town to know who I'm supporting. And believe it or not they're closing from seven-thirty until the games over. The whole town will be there tonight." She walks into our house and I close the door. Some moments I just want to stay in forever, this happens to be one of them.

"Hi, Mrs. Statemen" Whinny says to my mom. Whinny says she doesn't hold anything against my mom and has actually been really nice to her. But then again I'm not sure Whinny has it in her to be mean to anyone. I know she cut me out, but there was a force behind that.

"Hello, Whinny. How are you?"

"Pretty good" She looks at me and I put my arm around her.

"I know you're the one who helped get his mind back on the game Tuesday. Thank you for that. I think the whole town thanks you for that. I know this team has the potential to go to state. I still feel guilty for being the one to almost mess that up."

"I can read people pretty well. I just knew what he needed to hear to get focused again."

"It worked. Can I ask what you said? Or is that too much?"

"Mom"

"Sorry, too much"

"Michael likes to be a protector; I figured something along those lines might get his attention." Moms watching us both and I can see out of the corner of my eye she smiles. She can tell that with Whinny I'm the happiest I've been in months.

"I need to get going. I'll see you tonight sometime; remember to play with what's in here." She points her tiny finger to my heart. "You're going to do great."

"I don't want you to go."

"I know, but I have to, bye Mrs. Statemen, I guess I'll see you later as well."

"Bye Whinny, it was good to see you. You look cute." I walk her out the door, she starts to walk away when I grab her arm and turn her around and I kiss her. It's a kiss that takes the wind out me and makes my knees buckle. I can tell she feels the same thing.

"Okay then." She says afterwards.

"I love you."

She looks at me hard for a minute then softens "I love you too."

"I know we have only "technically" been together, what a week, but we've been hanging out since August and I know what we have is real and it's strong. You are my best friend."

She slowly starts to smile. "I'm proud of you Michael." She puts both hands on my arms and leans forward leaving a kiss on my check, then she turns and starts walking away.

"Do you want a ride?"

"What's my answer?"

"No." She smiles again and keeps walking. Whinny likes to walk places for the exercise and to just give her time to herself to think about things and just enjoy a few minutes of peacefulness. Well that and because she doesn't have a car.

I breathe in and out, the early November air leaving our breaths hanging in front of us. We've honestly played our hearts out tonight, me even running in for my own touchdown. It's the fourth quarter, and the last few seconds. All the defense has to do is stop them on this fourth down, then us offense heads in and takes a knee. The crowd is roaring with excitement, all of our fans just itching to run onto the field to congratulate us for making this a five-time sectional championship, as long as the defense can stop them now. Kevin and Lance come and stand next to me.

"They've got this."

"Hike!" Everyone is in motion. The quarterbacks got time, he's looking, and downfield is open.

"Holy shit" I say my heart starts to drop. Then like magic Joe comes flying around a tackle. He starts for the other teams' quarterback who is now on the move. Joe reaches him right as he releases the football. It's long, and gone. We all run down the side lines, the receiver jumps getting his fingers on the ball, but not quite all the way. It bounces out of bounds. The pass is incomplete. I pull my helmet on and summon the offense. One more play to make this official. The crowd is off the charts loud. My hearts pounding. We did it; we lead this team to victory.

"Hike!" I catch the ball and take a knee, and just like that, the games over, we start shaking hands with all the disheartened seniors from the other team and the younger ones too as the last few seconds of the clock wind down. Then the flood happens, the cheerleaders, the fans, the JV players, the coaches, all running towards us. I grab Kevin, Lance and Joe.

"Awesome tackle!"

"I wanted a win!"

"Atta boy!"

"Kevin!" Jamie makes her way through the crowd and he takes her in his arms. I've never seen him this happy. I make my way through the crazy throng of people and find our coaches.

"Thank you for pushing us so hard!" I yell over the still crazy loud crowd.

"This was all done by you guys. You worked hard for this, you deserve it!" He slaps me on the back. "But it's not over yet so you guys better be ready this coming week." I laugh.

"MICHAEL!" I turn around and see Whinny lifted in the air, Jimmy must be holding her like they do when they stunt. She's across the crowd from me.

"Hey let's help the boy out!" Someone hollers and they hoist me on their shoulders and everyone starts passing my across the field.

I've never crowd surfed before. Whinny starts laughing and watches as I move over the crowd closer to her, and then disappears from the air.

"Thanks everyone for supporting us all year long!" I yell as I'm passed along. Finally, I see Whinny and jump down. She jumps into my arms and wraps her legs around me.

"By far your best game of the year! I am so proud of you and the team!"

"We wouldn't be here if it wasn't for you. You helped me get my head out of my ass and concentrate on my team instead of just me." She smiles showing off all of her teeth.

"What are best friends for!?" And finally we kiss. As we do the whole crowd erupts into an even louder cheer. I smile and set her down, by far the best night of my life. I take Whinny's hand not wanting to lose her in the crowd and we make our way to some of our mutual friends. Everyone hugging everyone and being all excited.

Everyone starts winding down and moving off the field as the night goes on. We've already accepted our trophy and have gathered for team pictures.

"I can't believe we did it, we freakin' won." Lance says to us. He's smiling from ear to ear looking at Avery who's talking to Whinny and Jamie. She finally came to a game and surprisingly it looks like she's really enjoying herself. The cheerleaders are called over to take a picture with us. Whinny kneels down in front of me and Jamie in front of Kevin and the rest of the cheerleaders gather around finding spots in between us players.

"I'm just glad it's over, now we get a week before we have to start stressing out again." Parker remarks as cameras flash.

"Okay enough pictures can we please go change?"

"Alright you guys get out of here, let's give them a break." Coach says. We start heading back to the locker room to change.

"Hey Whinny." I grab her arm. "Thank you for everything."

"Michael." I lean in and give her a kiss on the cheek.

"Are you going to wait?"

"Yeah, I'll see you when you get out of the locker room."

As I head in I glance back to see Kevin walking around in the end zone. I head over to him.

"Well?" I ask

"Well I guess we're Sectional Champs." He smiles "another notch on the legend making belt."

I laugh, "Yeah, I guess so. So have you made your decision yet?" It's been out in the open for a while that Kevin has been looked at and watched by recruiters. It's changed everything for him.

"I have. What about you?"

"I'm pretty sure, it just feels right." We slap each other on the back and start walking towards the locker room.

"Woah, wait a minute." I say before we step off the field. "You like to be the last one to leave; I think you should give me a ten second head start."

"Whatever dude." He shoves me and we take off walking together. I glance back to see Whinny talking to my mom and Roger. She's the best support system I've ever had. I've made my decision on which school I'll be attending in the fall of next year, but I won't lie, the thought of being away from her scares the crap out of me.

Chapter Fifteen

So we won Sectionals, making in five straight sectional crowns, we won Regional's, first time in three years and we won Semi- State, first time our school has done that in ten years, we lost at state by two points. It really was bittersweet. It's hard to believe that I won't be playing football with all these guys ever again, but at least we went out with a bang and had done much better than last year. We are legends.

Today is actually graduation day, crazy to believe my senior year is over. It went by so fast, maybe because for once in my life I wasn't stressed about having to worry about anything, well for the majority of it, up until November it was kind of rough. I just concentrated on sports, school and of course my friends. This year was so much fun, all the journeys I've shared with these people. I've had some pretty good times, and some pretty bad, but I'll be walking away with great memories. I'm actually sad that it's over.

Our basketball season flew by and seemed really easy compared to everything we had just gone through with football workouts. I won the highest free throw percentage but other than that my season was pretty low key. But I also had officially signed to play football at college and to be the starting quarterback, as a freshman I'm really honored. They really didn't want me playing any more sports during the year, but since it was my senior year they let it go, as long as I didn't push it too hard. And I understood that if I got hurt my scholarship would be taken away. So I really didn't play much during the games.

But we won Sectionals and Regional's and lost first round at Semi-State. Whinny was there cheering on the sidelines the whole time, sadly with Jimmy. I'm still not comfortable with him getting to touch Whinny and technically getting to look up her skirt—even though she wears spanks—but I understand the nature of their relationship. I have to admit it's neat to watch them; they work together like a high performing machine. He can throw her in the air with one hand, she'll do some kind of flip and he'll catch her, then without setting her down he'll put her back up in a build. I even went to the cheerleading competition this year. Kevin, Kevin's mom, myself and my mom all went together. We were there to watch Jamie and of course Whinny. The cheerleaders won state making this number four in a row.

Christmas was pretty great too. I got Whinny some pearl earrings and a matching necklace. For mom I got a new toaster, it was kind of lame but she and I still weren't on the best terms. My mom got me my dad for Christmas. He came home for three days, it wasn't long but she and him had set everything up to surprise me, and it was a great surprise. We spent all three days together. He even got to meet Whinny and told me I did a great job. Whinny got me a whole bunch of new athletic shirts to wear to football practices next year. She special ordered them so they even have my future team's logo on them and my number.

Then believe it or not we hosted three charity events throughout the year. Whinny came up with the ideas and she had me, Kevin, Lance, Shane, Parker and Joe all there setting up and helping. We had a small in door carnival in the gym, almost like a pep rally on a Saturday for the whole community. We had a car wash in the spring and a bake sale. All three had great turnouts. Whinny was extremely excited that all of us guys helped her out. We donated our funds to Riley's Children Hospital, the Susan G. Komen fund for breast cancer and to the local Humane Society. Whinny really was making all of us better people and believe it or not, all of us guys had a great time at every event.

Track season came around I finally broke the school record in high jump but that was pretty much my only accomplishment there. Whinny does track too, which I never knew until this year. She pole vaults, usually clearing ten foot. She says she's good at it because of her cheerleading abilities. Then she also competes in the 1600-meter relay. It's been fun getting to go watch and support her instead of her always coming to support me. She actually made it all the way to state for pole vault. She vaulted twelve foot even and placed seventh overall. All of us guys made shirts for her and wore them at the state meet. Whinny's been around the guys most of the year and they've all come too really like her and she them. They were pretty pumped to make shirts with me. We even made up our own little cheers for her.

Whinny and I went to Prom together we went out with the whole group. Lance and Avery, Kevin and Jamie, Shane asked Penny, Parker and Lucy went together even though they broke up and Joe asked Lilly. We all went out to eat at the nicest restaurant in town. I couldn't keep my eyes off Whinny. She wore a gold dress that hugged her body down to her hips then flowed. She had a white bow that draped around her waist and fell into a train in the back. To me she looked like a model. We danced every song; all of us just had a great time. It was way better than last year's prom.

Lance and Avery actually won prom king and queen. I was glad it wasn't me and Whinny, we'd won homecoming king and queen, plus it was already tallied that we won class cutest couple. They were going to use the picture from our football sectional championship. It's where I'm holding Whinny and she's got her legs wrapped around me and we're both looking at each other and smiling from ear to ear. It looks pretty good with me in my uniform and her decked out in her ear head band, cheerleading sweat pants and my football jersey over her top. Neither of us even knew anyone had taken our picture in that moment, but to both of us it's our favorite because we weren't actually posing for the camera. We were just being us and being excited in the moment.

And speaking of class personalities Whinny won class Congeniality for the girls. And Simon won class congeniality for the guys. I've never talked to Simon but apparently he's pretty friendly.

Anyways after prom Whinny and I headed back to my house. We were going to get to be alone because mom was helping out at post prom. I helped Whinny change out of her dress and I thought we were going to; well go all the way I guess to put it.

"Michael." She said.

"Yes." We were lying in bed, me on top of her. I had her head cradled in my arms and I was running my nose across her face.

"I don't want to do this yet." I lift my head back and stare into her eyes.

"We don't have to do anything." I kiss her jawbone. "You know I've never done this before either."

"You haven't?"

"No, Jasmine and I came close, but I never felt the connection, I never wanted her to be my first."

"But you were together for so long."

"That doesn't mean it was a good time together. We fought almost all the time; I couldn't stand the thought of giving myself to someone who made me feel five inches tall. Most guys don't think like I do. They just would have gone ahead and did the crap out of her, but I knew it wouldn't have been fair to her."

Whinny leans up and kisses me. She runs her hands through my hair and pulls me closer to her. I wrap my arms tighter around her back. She's so small that I can touch all the way up to both my biceps with her wrapped up in them.

"I love you Whinny." I kiss her nose.

"I love you too." She smiles.

We then got ready for post prom. I won two hundred dollars and somehow Whinny won four hundred. She cleaned up the place. Everyone was tired and ready to head home and sleep. We got one huge group photo of us all with our prize winnings, and then headed out. Even though things didn't go exactly as planned it was still by far the best night I could have asked for, lying next to Whinny almost naked pretty much set all of me on fire. Yeah prom was great. Plus, she did end up staying the night with me, and getting to lay all night next to her was the next best thing.

Mom and I finally sat down and talked after Christmas. After she set everything up to have dad come see me, I knew it was time for forgiveness, I understood what Whinny had meant, that in the long run forgiveness is everything. Dad wasn't mad or hostile at mom, so I realized I shouldn't be either. I then understood what she was saying about being lonely and having someone care for you and to take that loneliness away. She and Roger agreed they don't want to get married, at least for a while. They actually aren't living together either; they agreed to wait until I move away to college since I'm still not thrilled about the whole thing. Mom gave birth to a beautiful little girl the very end of April, actually a week after prom. They named her Ruby, and they will all be attending my graduation ceremony here in a bit.

Dad came back from overseas in April and got himself a small cottage close to the ocean. He isn't finished with active duty though and none of us are sure how long he'll be here. He and mom have been great together, as far as getting along. He was even there for Ruby's birth. He says he doesn't blame mom for giving up on him and wanting a more stable and compatible partner. He will also be attending my graduation. He will also probably move closer to my college so he can come to as many games as possible since he missed all of my senior year. I will officially be the starting quarterback for my new school, the University of Tennessee. I can't begin to describe how excited I am to be playing where Peyton Manning did.

As for Kevin, well he and Jamie have been an item ever since our fall dance. She is the first girl I've seen him stay with and actually be serious about their relationship. I can tell he's pretty into her and she's never looked at Taz again. Ironic though, Taz broke up with the popular girl trying to get Jamie's attention. She wanted nothing to do with him. Kevin also got a scholarship to play football at college. He and I will be playing on the same team. And no we didn't plan on that happening, it just did. I know he's sad to be leaving Jamie, but I think they'll be okay. She's pretty crazy about him and she's down to earth and sweet. He'll never have to worry about her trust. They've both decided they want to try the long distance and see how it goes. When I say long distance I really mean 7 hours.

Whinny and I have also been together ever since the night of the fall dance. We've spent this whole year together, as just stated above. She really has helped me through, even more than I sometimes realize. I've never loved or cared for another person as much as I do for her. Through the course of this year I've made sure that we've taken lots of photos together, and for her graduation gift I put together a photo album of our senior year together. I've helped her out with studying and bringing her homework when she misses school, and occasionally I'd chip in and give her some of the money I made over the summer. Of course she'd never take it, she's too proud, but I always found a way to secretly help her. Mom apologized time and time again to Whinny, they've been best friends ever since. Mom really does love Whinny being around. Some nights when she'd be off work Whinny would come over and make dinner for us and we'd all sit down and eat as a family. I can tell it's really helped her too. For once in her life she has a family, people who need her, and love her.

Speaking of families, Whinny wasn't lying about hers. Her grandparents decided to move once Whinny turned eighteen. After all that's only how long they needed to provide for her. They officially moved to Florida, and Whinny stayed living here in the house until May, as of now it's on the market, but Whinny will be moving in about a month in a half to head to school so she said she didn't mind. The only nice thing they did was leave Whinny with a car, so she can get to college, and leave her ten thousand dollars for when she starts school, which was very nice but other than that they pretty much disappeared. They left a couple numbers with her but that was it, they disappeared into the evening without a care of what they were leaving behind.

My heart went out to Whinny and I know at times she hurts more than others, but she never really lets it show. For the rest of the summer until she leaves for school, she'll be staying here with me and sometimes with my dad—who's a big fan of hers too.

I can honestly say I'm beyond nervous because today Whinny is finally going to tell me where she's going to college. She wouldn't tell me even after I signed. She said she didn't want either of us thinking about it. And really I'm surprised Jimmy has kept quiet this long about it too, but not one peep of where they're going have I heard.

I can't imagine going anywhere without her. I'm more than positive that we can make a long distance relationship work as far as how we feel about each other. It's just I know we're both going to have conflicting schedules with her cheerleading and me playing ball.

Jasmine stayed single throughout the year, even though she was happy for me and Whinny she still would give me a hard time about being in a relationship. She didn't want to admit that Whinny and I were happier than she and I, but after several talks Jasmine finally told me she thought we made a cute couple and if I was happy then she was. I even heard that she settled on a school. She was offered a position on Dukes cheerleading squad, I'm not sure if it's a scholarship or just something for her to do, but she's happy.

All of us have made commitments to schools. Lance and Avery will be attending the same college in the fall. They're headed to the University of North Carolina, located in Chapel Hill, about three hours from here. They're very excited to be going together. They've actually made a pretty great couple. Lance was able to get her away from the crowd that was always doing the drugs and she became part of ours. She even started coming to events like basketball games, and she seemed to be enjoying herself.

Joe and Parker decided on the same school too, North Carolina State University in Raleigh and Shane is going as a walk on to play basketball at Duke, in Durham. All three schools are located about thirty minutes from each other so I'm sure they will all stay in touch. Kevin and I, well we'll be five hours away from them, seven from home, we're headed to Knoxville, Tennessee. We're excited though; this is the time of our lives.

"Michael, we need to get going." I glance at myself in the mirror one last time. Hair's still shaggy but a little shorter, and I look pretty much the exact same as I did the first day of school. Only now I don't feel so alone or worried or scared of what the future is going to hold. I feel confident and beyond lucky to have the life I do. I pick up my robe, hat and tassel and go downstairs. Mom starts to tear up. "I can't believe you're graduating today."

"This is such a big accomplishment Michael; you should be proud." Roger says. I'm still not a big fan of him, but I'm trying for mom.

"Thanks, and I appreciate you two coming." Mom and Roger have been to every event of mine since football Sectionals. It's been weird but nice. I watch as mom loads Ruby into the car seat.

"I'm headin' out, see y'all there." I get in my truck and drive to the school for the last time. The thought is actually very bittersweet. Whinny said she'd meet me here; I can't stop thinking about her. I will be leaving right after the fourth of July to get settled in and start practicing. I only have one more month with her and I want to make it the best month I can.

I park, and see Kevin, Jamie, Lance and Avery. Parker's here and single, along with Shane, and Joe.

"I can't believe today's the day." I say giving each one of them a high five.

"Michael, are you ready for the University of Tennessee!? I can't believe we're going to be playing at Neyland Stadium!"

I laugh "it's a great feeling." Kevin and I actually signed the same day to play football. It wasn't until that very morning when we were looking in the conference room that we noticed only one team's head coach was there. Kevin and I looked at each other and said "no way" at the same time. The head coach loved how well he and I play together so he was pretty pumped when we both decided that's where we want to go.

"Hey good looking" Whinny saunters over from out of nowhere. We kiss and everything in the world feels right. I wrap my arms around her and embrace her in a hug. For the rest of the time we have together I'm not letting her go.

"So when are you going to tell me? I'm dying to know." All the others are watching us too. I know Avery and Jamie both know where Whinny's going but everyone else has been kept in the dark.

"I know you are. After the ceremony before we take off to graduation parties, you are taking me back to your house and taking me up in that tree house. That's where I'll tell you."

"Seriously, that's where you want me to take you? And you're making me wait even longer?"

"Yes" she smiles at me and kisses my bottom lip "and because it kind of means a lot to me."

"Okay then."

"Alright graduates let's line up!" Jamie hugs Kevin and heads to find a seat. The rest of us start walking towards the football field. We've been a pretty close group of friends, and to be honest the girls being around has actually made us closer. This year really has been the best senior year a guy could ask for.

As we stand waiting to be placed in order I take Whinny's hand. I feel bad for her that she has no family here, besides mine, but she doesn't seem to mind at least not at this particular moment.

"Whinny, no matter where you go, no matter how far I'll always love you. You'll always be the one who has my heart."

She squeezes my hand as a tear runs down her check. "And you'll always be here for me? Always have my back?" She smiles

"Always."

"Good, I love you too."

Hope you enjoyed The Leather, The Lace, Life's Sweet Embrace by Ky Rose!

Please check out
http://www.dreambigpublishing.net/
for more info on the books in our collection.

58636365R00105

Made in the USA
Charleston, SC
14 July 2016